Amish Christmas Memories

Terri Downes

Published by Trellis Publishing, 2021.

AMISH CHRISTMAS MEMORIES

First edition. July 14, 2021.

Copyright © 2021 Terri Downes.

ISBN: 979-8224998524

Written by Terri Downes.

AMISH CHRISTMAS MEMORIES

TERRI DOWNES

Most of the time, Martin was glad that Julia had come to work for him. *Most* of the time.

Martin glanced dubiously up at the dark clouds as he walked away from the store. Would it really snow, he wondered... it was only the beginning of December, and the winter had begun mildly. Still, the metallic tang in the air suggested that a dusting might be on its way.

Looking back at the furniture store, Martin could see Julia through the lighted window. She looked completely calm, arranging a set of stools near the counter, as though she had entirely forgotten their argument.

She was good at that, Martin thought. Keeping focused on the task at hand. This was one of the reasons he was *usually* glad he had hired her. In their small Plain community, most women of her age were married with families. Julia was still single at twenty-seven, and showed no desire to change this. Instead, she was dedicated to her work at the store, which was gratifying.

On the other hand, she had now dedicated herself to such an extent that she had started arguing with Martin about the business. Some of her ideas were fine, but some were entirely too ambitious.

This afternoon, she had insisted that the best way to increase Martin's customer base was to start selling at those awful markets they put on for tourists, where everything was overpriced and looked the same.

"You're the one who keeps saying you want to expand," she had pointed out.

"Not if it means compromising the work," he had retorted. "This is my family's business. I'd rather keep it small than ruin it. Doesn't your family have any traditions?"

She had then done what she always did when an argument became personal. She backed down, lowering her eyes and saying *it doesn't matter, never mind.* She then returned to her duties with the air of someone who had never had an opinion in their life. Martin had not meant for this to happen, and half wished she had continued to argue just so he would not feel guilty afterward.

"*Daed*!"

Martin turned toward the shout and waved at the twins as they approached with their grandmother. As he stood at the end of the land waiting for them, he looked back once more at the store, wondering what their mother would have made of Julia.

He placed a hand against his chest for a moment, as he felt the slight pain that often accompanied an unexpected memory of Sadie. Three years after her death, it had become easier to think about her in passing, but the longing for her worsened during winter. She had always started glowing when the cold came, her cheeks red and her eyes sparkling, looking forward to Christmas.

If she had been here, now, she would already be making meal plans and Christmas cards. She would be counting down the days along with the children.

If Sadie was here, Martin thought, she probably would have had a long talk with Julia, making friends, so Julia knew she could offer her opinions without confrontation. Something Martin would not know how to do even if someone gave him step-by-step instructions.

Martin tried to let the frown fall from his face as Simon and Aaron reached him, having far outstripped Martin's mother as they ran down the lane.

"Are you done?" asked Aaron excitedly. "We want to get home before the snow."

"We're going to pile it up in the yard so we can slide down it," added Simon.

"You'll have to wait till it falls first," said Martin. He bent down to redo the crooked buttons on Simon's coat.

"Are you done already?" asked his mother, as she reached the little group. "I thought you had to finish your inventory."

"Julia's doing that," said Martin, struggling to straighten up as Aaron climbed onto his back. "She offered to close up."

"I don't know what you would do without her," smiled his mother, who had nagged him to get an assistant for six months before he finally hired Julia. "We'll have to have her at the house one of these days."

"Sure," said Martin.

He imagined his mother inviting Julia to their chaotic family home, where Martin's brother, sister-in-law and their three children lived, alongside Martin, the six-year-old twins and his mother. He was fairly certain that the calm and collected Julia would – very politely – refuse.

***

Julia stepped closer to the little wood burning stove near the store entrance, holding her hands out to warm them. Martin had argued with her over its necessity, and Julia had assumed that he would have his way. This morning, however, she had arrived to find that he had installed it over the weekend.

He had said nothing about it, so neither had she – and she had been very careful not to look triumphant when the first two customers through the door mentioned how nice and welcoming it felt.

There was a loud crash at the back of the store. Julia turned to see one of the tables on its side, with Aaron and Simon looking at it guiltily.

"We were playing at being cats," Simon explained, as his father came running in from the workshop.

"Cats climb on things," added Aaron defensively.

"And cats land on their feet when they fall," said Martin sharply, righting the table. "You won't. I've told you before about this."

"Sorry, *Daed*," Simon and Aaron chorused.

The boys wandered over to stand next to Julia as their father lectured them about staying safe. Julia felt bad for the young twins. She wondered why Martin was so strict; the boys weren't that bad. A little mischievous, perhaps.

Every other time she saw the twins, they were plastered with mud or paint, the white blond hair they had inherited from Martin tousled like pale straw. But they were always cheerful, always having fun, and always apologetic when they did wrong.

She wished she could play with them the way she used to play with her younger siblings up in North Brook. She had loved making her little sister and brothers laugh; it had been the only comfort during the years of endless, grinding responsibility following their parents' deaths.

"Don't stand so close to the stove, boys," Martin said, just as it seemed his lecture might be coming to an end.

"Julia's standing close," complained Simon, as Julia took a guilty step backward.

"Julia is a grown up," said Martin.

The boys looked up at Julia as though expecting her to share a conspiratorial smile with them, but she quickly moved away to the counter.

Martin walked by on his way back out to the workshop, pausing at the counter.

"I can keep an eye on them, if they want to play in here," Julia could not help offering, even as she tried to make it sound as though it didn't matter.

"It's fine. They have school work to do." Martin frowned. "I don't want them disturbing you."

I don't mind, Julia almost said. It was on the tip of her tonuge. But Martin's direct gaze shut the words down. He was paying her to work in the store, not take care of his children. That was the way it should be.

"Of course," she said quickly, looking away.

Martin gave instructions to the boys and left.

However much she wished to have the boys like her, she knew it would not be worth going down that route again.

You can't borrow someone else's family, she reminded herself. She took out the letter she had received that morning from her sister in North Brook, and stared down at it. It should serve as a reminder, she thought, of the pain that came from forgetting your place.

This was why she had already refused two invitations from Martin's mother, Ellie. Julia had come up with excuses both times, knowing she would have to accept sooner or later so as not to seem rude.

It would have been so difficult to explain the real reason she did not want to go to Martin's home. She hated being around large families. It was hard enough living alone in her little cottage, with not a soul to speak to every morning and evening. It was downright unbearable being around others who had what she longed for, reminding her of everything she lacked.

The bell over the shop door rang out. Julia looked up and sighed inwardly. Ellie, Martin's mother, was coming in with one of her friends. No doubt to make another offer, and this time Julia would have to accept.

"Julia, isn't it?" said the other woman, walking forward with a kind smile. "I'm Miriam."

"Oh yes – you're the schoolmistress," Julia remembered.

"I am." Miriam tilted her head. "You haven't been in Lancaster long, have you?"

"Just a few months," said Julia. "But I used to live here. My family moved away when I was a child."

"Are you enjoying being back?"

Julia hesitated. Enjoy was a strong word. She had felt exhilarated, on her return, but it was mostly because she knew she would finally have a fresh start, away from the mire of troubled relationships she had left behind in North Brook.

"It's lovely to work here," she said finally.

"Julia's just about running the whole business," said Ellie from where she was standing by the stove.

Julia tried to protest this, particularly when Martin appeared from within the workshop. She didn't want him to think she was trying to take over.

However, Ellie started listing the changes Julia had put in place since she started, and how she had reorganized everything from the order sheets to the stockroom.

Martin could not disagree, although he did frown a lot, leaning against the counter with his back partially turned to Julia. Miriam, on the other hand, looked impressed.

"I can see why you recommended her," she said to Ellie.

"Recommended me?" Julia frowned. "For what?"

"We've had some trouble organizing the Christmas program," said Miriam. "I've been ill for a few months, and my replacement was supposed to get things started without me, but she didn't manage."

"But there are only a few weeks until Christmas," said Julia, remembering how long the programs often took to rehearse and arrange. "Have you nothing prepared at all?"

"Almost nothing," said Miriam. "I've never had to run the program by myself before, either. Ellie thought you might be able to help out."

"I thought you were going to your family over Christmas?" said Martin, looking back at Julia, his brows slightly lowered.

Julia flushed. She closed her fist under the counter, crumpling the letter from her sister.

"I said I might go to visit. But I can easily stay and help." Julia tried to smile. "I used to help with the programs at North Brook, when my brothers and sister were little."

"Wonderful," said Miriam, smiling broadly, her relief evident. "That's two so far then."

"Two?"

"Martin's already agreed to make the sets."

Julia tried to keep her smile in place. It was difficult enough dealing with Martin at work, when he was in charge. She could only imagine what it would be like trying to *organize* him. No doubt this was why he did not want her to help, preferring that she went away to her family.

Well, there was little chance of that.

***

Martin thought it a little much that he should be expected to spend extra time with someone he was not really friends with. Not that he disliked Julia, but their relationship had been tenuous ever since she started working for him. How could you be close friends with an employee?

Besides which, and despite his efforts to ignore it, Martin was always vaguely aware of the fact that Julia was a single woman. And a very pretty one. He almost had not hired her, worried that people would think he wanted her around for her looks.

In the end, of course, her appearance hardly mattered, given how good she was at keeping a professional distance between them.

Which was why, as they set off toward the school together for the first Christmas program rehearsal, Martin felt quite awkward.

I should probably make some sort of conversation, he thought, hunching into his coat as a cold wind whipped up around them. Otherwise they would be walking in silence for half an hour.

"It's very good of you to help Miriam," he said.

"You're helping too," Julia replied. "And your sacrifice is much greater, agreeing to close the store for the afternoon."

"But the boys are in the program," Martin said. "The school often expects parents to help out. For you it seems more like an act of charity."

Julia's expression tightened slightly. Martin wondered, belatedly, whether she would be offended at a reminder of her single status.

"I like to keep busy." Julia tucked the ends of her scarf into her coat to stop them from flying about.

"Of course." Martin tried again. "But you could have gone home to your family."

"Actually, I couldn't." Julia's expression remained still, as though frozen in the cold air. "My sister is spending Christmas with her husband's parents, my youngest brother has a newborn to take care of, and my other brother is in the middle of building an extension onto his house."

"I'm sure they'd make space for you if you asked," said Martin, thinking about how many relations they managed to cram into his parents' big farm house every Christmas.

Julia did not respond. After a moment, Martin had a sudden, awful suspicion that she had already asked, and been refused.

Why do I keep saying the wrong thing? He wished he could kick himself.

He also wished, for the first time he could remember, that he was actually friends with Julia. He could have asked her about her family, and told her that it was their loss if they didn't want her around.

Instead, he started on a different track, telling her about some absurd game the twins had invented the day before. It had involved climbing up and down the stairs using only the bannisters.

Julia seemed happy to let the conversation focus on the boys. In fact, Martin was surprised at the way her comments showed how much she had been paying attention to them. She seemed to remember so many small details that Martin imagined only he knew, about their likes and dislikes and little adventures.

The conversation shortened the journey, and they soon arrived at the little school hall, where Martin was greeted by both twins flying at him at once.

Martin caught a small smile from Julia before she headed inside. As she turned away, her face fell into sadness. Martin could imagine how it would feel, having been brushed aside by her own family, to see such affection up close. He wished he could tell the boys to go hug her as well.

By the time he got inside, Julia had already taken charge, and was directing the older children to move the desks to the sides of the room. A cluster of mothers were standing by the door, clucking with concern.

One of them, a reedy woman named Iris whom Martin had never particularly liked, reached over and clutched at Julia's sleeve as she passed.

"Listen, I know Miriam put you in charge of the rehearsals," she said, her thin smile stretching in an overly-sweet manner. "But you've no children of your own, so you might have a little trouble with getting them under control. Don't worry about asking for help."

Julia looked quietly at Iris before answering. Martin recognized her expression as one worn during the many times they had argued about something.

"Thank you," she said. "I'll bear that in mind."

"I'm sure Julia can manage," Martin said. He felt the gazes of all the women on him at once and half wanted to run back out of the door. He cleared his throat. "She's helped with a lot of programs before – haven't you?"

Julia nodded. She was still maintaining careful control over her expression, but there was a hint of a smile there.

"And she might not have her own children, but she raised her younger siblings by herself. I'd say that gives her plenty of experience."

The mothers seemed pacified at this, and went back to their cluster. Julia, on the other hand, looked genuinely surprised that Martin remembered so much about her.

"Thank you," she said quietly.

"Don't worry about them," said Martin, glancing at the group of women. "They just worry too much, sometimes. Some of them take a while to warm up... and some of them just like to complain."

Julia stifled a laugh.

"You don't have to stay too long," she said. "Just until we've worked out which scenes we're going to do, so you know what sets we need."

"I'll stay till the end," said Martin. "I already took the afternoon off, and I'd need to come back for the boys anyway."

"I can walk them home if you like," said Julia.

"Or we could walk you home," suggested Martin. "I'd just as soon tire them out after they get all excited at the rehearsal."

"That's probably a good idea."

Martin smiled at Julia. Perhaps they were better friends than they realized.

***

"Julia, can't we practice again?"

"You know it off by heart," Julia said, shaking her head and laughing as Aaron tried to make puppy-dog pleading eyes at her from the other side of the counter.

For all her efforts to keep her distance from the twins, she had not counted on how excited they would be over their parts in the Christmas program. With the hours she spent with them at school, and at the store, they now seemed to have adopted her as a constant companion.

She had even started looking after them while Martin was away from the store. It went against all the rules she had set, but she convinced herself that it was alright – it was just to help with the program. Things would go back to normal after Christmas.

"If you want to practice, go do it with your brother," she said.

Aaron turned away with an air of deep disappointment, before forgetting his misery and bounding away to join Simon.

Julia wanted to play with them, but was mindful of the work that still needed to be done. And even though it was nice to be more free and easy with the twins, she had to be careful not to get too close. She did not want them to start seeing her as a member of the family – more importantly, she did not want to start seeing herself as that.

She chuckled as the twins jumped up onto a bench to use as a stage, going through the lines of one of their skits with extra loud enunciation and large hand gestures.

Neither she, nor the boys, noticed Martin entering with his mother. They did hear his voice cutting across the recital, however.

"Boys."

He did not shout, but his tone was unmistakably stern. The twins stopped and stared at him for a moment before jumping back down.

"So you do remember that I have told you not to climb on the furniture," said Martin.

Julia flushed. She had remembered, but had not thought to enforce what had always seemed an overly harsh rule.

"We had to make a stage!" protested Aaron.

"Julia was helping us practice," said Simon.

Julia felt vaguely betrayed by this passing of blame, but knew she was at fault.

"I'm sorry," she said at once. "I should have reminded them."

Martin glanced at her, but continued to talk to the boys.

"If you can't behave yourselves while you're here, you'll have to go home with your grandmother."

Despite their loud and tearful protests, the twins were soon on their way back to the farmhouse. Ellie tutted at them as they put their coats on. She also gave Julia a slightly strange look – almost sympathetic, Julia thought, although she could not imagine why.

Martin watched them head up the lane before turning back to face Julia. She could tell he was disappointed. She could read him better, now – they had been becoming friends, these past weeks, spending hours outside work at rehearsals, or walking to and from the school.

Julia often reminded herself to hold back from any real, intimate friendship, knowing it could not lead anywhere. She felt confused and

guilty every time she found herself looking forward to spending time with Martin.

Now, she felt guilty for a different reason.

"I'm sorry," Julia said again, biting her lip. "They didn't seem to be doing any harm."

"No, but I had told them before not to do that," said Martin.

"Yes, I know."

Julia looked down at her work. This was what she got for involving herself. The boys did not belong to her, and she had no right to behave as though they did. She had no right to feel sad that they were being taken home.

Their home, not hers. Julia's home was hers alone.

She expected Martin to go back to the workshop. After a moment, however, she heard him walk back over from the door and stop and the counter. When she raised her head, he was looking directly at her, his expression softer than it had been.

"You must think I'm very strict with them," he said.

"Not too strict. Or not all the time, anyway," replied Julia. Then she quickly added, "Besides, it doesn't matter what I think, I've no right to – "

"The problem is that I wasn't strict with them at all, for a long time," said Martin, gently interrupting Julia's attempt to distance herself.

"What do you mean?" asked Julia, her work forgotten.

"When Sadie passed away, we moved back into my parent's house. To begin with, I wanted nothing more than to forget that I was a father. I left the burden of care on my parents – but they didn't have the energy to handle three year old twins." Martin looked down for a moment, frowning at the memory. "It took a year for me to find myself again. And by then, the twins were used to having their own way pretty much all the time."

"You had to start from scratch," said Julia, finally understanding the hard line Martin took with the boys. "That must have been challenging."

"Very." Martin smiled wryly. "Discipline is hard at the best of times."

"I know. I struggled to get my siblings to obey me, after my parents passed," said Julia.

Martin looked a little surprised at the admission. Julia felt surprised at herself; she normally avoided any mention of her family.

Why was she sharing so much with Martin? And why was she so eager to hear the details of his life? Julia had the sudden sensation of walking down a steep slope, her feet speeding up without her permission.

"Do you miss them?" Martin asked quietly.

"Sometimes," said Julia.

Her heart was beating fast, warning her away from something. *This is not for you. This is not what happens to you. You do not get the things you want.*

She cleared her throat and placed her hand on the papers in front of her.

"Right now I'm too busy to miss anyone."

Martin stepped away as she closed the door on their conversation.

"Of course," he said. "What time do we need to be at the school?"

"Six."

"Alright."

And despite every reprimand she had offered herself in the last few minutes, Julia could not help but smile as she looked forward to their walk together.

***

The sets had been finished a week ago, as had the new benches that Martin had designed for the choral singing. He had no real reason to keep going to the program rehearsals.

And yet here he was, a few days from the performance, spending yet another afternoon in the school hall. He had let himself get dragged into more and more little jobs here and there, until it hardly seemed to matter that the job he had actually been asked to do was done.

Right now, he was fixing a wobbly table at the back of the schoolroom. It was technically still related to the program – it would be used for snacks served to the parents after the performances were done – but Martin still felt as though he would not be able to explain to anyone why he was here, if they asked.

Perhaps the Christmas spirit had overtaken him. The boys had been growing more excited by the day, and no doubt their enthusiasm would have some effect.

Martin watched the twins tear across the hall, almost knocking down two small girls who were carrying armfuls of paper streamers. He was about to go and tell them to calm down, but Julia called out first.

"Aaron, Simon, slow down, please. It's no good pulling those faces at me, I'm not asking you to walk across hot coals."

The boys sighed and settled down to run lines with a few friends. Martin felt pleased. Julia had been paying closer attention to the boys' needs since their talk.

He could tell it was a little hard for her – she loved having the children see her almost as a playmate, and relied on them obeying her from sheer force of friendliness. But she also understood that the twins needed discipline, just like they would need to take an unpleasant tasting medicine, and she was doing her best to provide it.

Martin had not realized he was looking at Julia, until she looked over at him. She tilted her head, as though expecting him to say something or ask a question. Before Martin could think of anything to say, one of the children started crying.

Julia went to the small girl at once, kneeling down beside her and asking what the matter was. As far as Martin could tell through the wailing, the issue was that the little girl's hat was too big for her.

He hid a smile, thinking of how seriously all the children were taking the program. This morning, the boys had spent half an hour sketching their plans for the cookies they were supposed to decorate and give to the parents after the performance.

"We're supposed to wear the hats in the funny song, and now I can't," wept the girl, holding out the offending headwear.

Julia took it from her and looked at it gravely. "Too big, you say? Are you sure?"

She put the hat on. It immediately sank over her eyes.

"No, I'm pretty sure it's supposed to look like this," she said, over the laughter of the children watching.

"But you can't see anything!" said the little girl.

"What? Who said that?" asked Julia, whipping her head around.

Martin could not stop himself from laughing along with the children. Julia pulled the hat off, her expression still completely serious.

"You may have a point," she told the little girl, who was now giggling as well. "Why don't we use some of the leftover paper from the streamers to pad out the band?"

They settled on one of the desks near to where Martin was working. He found himself listening to their chatter. It was quite sweet, hearing Julia talk to the girl in that way she had, of making every child feel they were just as important as an adult.

Then it stopped being sweet, and became sad.

The girl started telling Julia all about her older brothers and sisters, who were coming to see her in the program. Julia's responses became quieter and quieter.

"Do you have brothers and sisters?" the girl asked eventually.

"Two brothers and one sister," said Julia shortly. "There now, I think that should keep the hat up. Why don't you go and practice that song with the others?"

Martin watched Julia's shoulders slump as the girl ran off. She seemed to sense his gaze and turned.

"I can't help feeling angry at your family," he said, before he even knew he was going to say it.

"Why?" she asked, her voice dull.

"After everything you did for them," he said. "Now they don't even offer to have you home for Christmas."

Julia flinched a little. She never shared that much, but Martin had picked up a few things about Julia's past. She had taken care of her siblings for ten years, since she was sixteen, working two jobs at a time to keep them fed and sheltered.

She had obviously not had time for courting, and so had stayed single, giving up a chance at her own family. Then her siblings had all married, one by one, leaving her alone.

"They want to have normal families," said Julia, looking out at the various groups of children scattered around the hall. "Being with me reminds them of how difficult it was for them, growing up."

"It was difficult for you too, surely."

"Yes. But I became the parent. They don't see me as the same as them. When my sister got married, I stayed with her for a while, and then with one of my brothers, then the other. But it just felt like I was intruding."

"How do you know?"

"Well, for one thing, my sister said that I was intruding," said Julia, her mouth flattening into a bitter smile.

"That's terrible."

"She was right," said Julia. "She had a baby, and I kept trying to take care of him. I was so used to being the parent that I couldn't stop. But I was never a real parent, I was just pretending. And now they don't need me to pretend any more."

Martin could not think of anything to say, watching with a pain in his chest as Julia carefully blinked back her tears.

"It doesn't matter all that much," she said after a moment. "They couldn't have me *home* for Christmas, anyhow. My home is here."

"Yes, it is," said Martin.

The pain in his chest softened as he looked at her, turning into something else. Something warm, and alive.

After a moment he realized, half with fear and half with joy, what the feeling was. As Julia rose to go back to the children, Martin could not think of what the moment had been, when he had started to fall in love with her. But it was done.

He had finished with the table, but he did not make a move to go. He would find something else to do. There was no way he was leaving now.

***

Despite her close involvement with the Christmas program for the last few weeks, Julia had not really felt as though she was in a festive mood. She had enjoyed spending time with the children, but had used this as a distraction from the fact that it was Christmas more than anything else.

Tonight, on Christmas Eve, she was walking to the school for the program performance. It was the first time in a while, she realized, that she was walking anywhere by herself. Martin was driving over with his family. The twins were already at the school, along with all the children who were decorating cookies for their parents. And as Julia walked, alone, she finally felt that old familiar Christmas thrill.

It was partly due to the light dusting of snow that had appeared in answer to the twins' fervent prayers. The sight of the school hall, windows lit and shining against the dark hills and slate gray sky, also looked like something out of a story.

Julia suddenly felt so very grateful that she had been able to do this. She may not have had any family of her own, but this project had let her feel part of the community in a way that it might have taken years to achieve. She could already see a couple of women waving to her from the school porch – the mothers who had helped with the program, now warmed to her as much as if she had grown up here.

Perhaps it was the feeling of friendship, or the lights, or the warmth inside the school hall, or the excitement in the air – but when Martin waved Julia over to sit with him and his family, she did not even hesitate.

She grinned at him as the program started, with Miriam introducing the first song. Martin smiled at her in the half-dark.

Julia had been so caught up in the evening that she was completely unprepared for the sudden fluttering sensation that rose up as the two of them shared a smile.

She tried to ignore it and pay attention to the stage. But when the twins finished their skit, she found herself sharing another grin with Martin. She saw the look of pride on his face, and felt it on her own – but that was not how it should be. She should be no more proud of the twins than any of the other children she had worked with.

She turned to face the front again quickly.

Although there was plenty of room between their chairs, she shifted away slightly. Martin did not seem to notice, but Julia could feel Ellie looking at her. She wondered, belatedly, what Ellie would think about Julia coming to sit with them as though she was one of the family.

The rest of the program passed by much more quickly than Julia had expected. In her whirling thoughts, everything seemed dizzyingly fast, and before she knew it she was standing up with everyone else as they sang the last song.

As the song ended, and a buzz of conversation rose around her, Julia slipped between the chairs to the side of the room. She wanted nothing more than to run out of the school room, and away from her fear. But before she could get more than a few steps toward the door, Simon had rushed up to her and hugged her. Aaron followed, hugging her from the other side.

"You did so well!" she said, trying to make her voice as cheerful as it should be. Even if she was miserably confused, they boys deserved her support.

"Come on, come to the back table," said Aaron, grabbing hold of her hand and tugging at it.

"What for?" Julia laughed as Simon started tugging on her other hand.

"We all decorated cookies for our parents," said Simon.

"That's lovely," said Julia, looking around to see where Martin had got to. "I think your *daed* went to help move those chairs –"

"But we made one for you as well!" beamed Aaron.

"One each," corrected Simon. "So you'll have two."

Julia felt as though there was something stuck at the back of her throat.

"But they're for your parents," she said, barely able to get the words out. "I'm – I'm not – your – "

"You kind of are our *mamme*," said Simon.

"Almost completely," agreed Aaron.

They both looked so happy about this that it was all Julia could do to keep herself from crying right in front of them. She needed to get away.

"That's so sweet of you," she managed. "I just need to go do something very quickly – why don't you give them to your *daed* first."

She smiled at the boys as she moved away, hoping she had not disappointed them, turning quickly toward the door. She bumped into someone in her haste.

"Julia?" It was Miriam, her face creased with worry. "Are you alright?"

"I'm fine, I just – it's a little warm, I need some air."

Julia brushed past her and headed for the porch. There were a few parents there – she smiled and thanked them as they congratulated her on the program, hurrying down the steps as soon as she could.

She slipped around the side of the building, hoping no-one wondered where she was going. As soon as she was alone, she leaned back against the wall of the schoolhouse, forcing herself to take deep, slow breaths.

Her tear-filled eyes felt unnaturally hot against the ice in the air. She looked up at the sky, now clear of its clouds, allowing the half-moon to light up the snowy ground.

Julia could hear talking and laughter inside. She gritted her teeth.

She had done it again. She had let herself pretend that she was part of something, that she had been given a role she had no real right to. She was not part of Martin's family. However close she allowed herself to get to them, it would just hurt all the more when they moved on.

When she heard footsteps crunching toward her in the snow, Julia swiftly wiped her tears away and started back the way she had come, not wanting anyone to ask questions. She halted in her tracks when she saw Martin.

He kept walking until he was just a foot away, then stood looking at her carefully.

"Miriam told me you headed outside," he said.

Julia swallowed, unable to come up with any excuse. He could obviously tell she had been crying.

Martin held something out. Two cookies, decorated to within an inch of their lives.

"They did tell me which was which," he said, "but I can't remember. I think Simon made the one with the snowflake thing."

Julia made no move to take them.

"They'll be very hurt if you don't," said Martin gently.

Julia held out her hand and took them quickly, as though she was afraid of burning herself.

"I never meant – " her voice wobbled. "I didn't mean to – "

"You didn't mean for them to love you?" asked Martin.

"Do they – do they?" Julia almost gasped, feeling as though her chest was about to crack open. "Don't tell me that. I can't hear that."

"Why not?"

"Because I can't want this." Julia squeezed her eyes shut for a second. "I'm always wanting things I can't have. My whole life."

Would he be able to tell that she meant him as well? Julia risked looking back up at Martin. His gaze was still steadily on her.

"Is this something you can't have?" His voice was soft and subdued. "Seems like something you have already."

"They said – I was almost their mother." Julia nearly choked on the word, feeling as though she was making a confession. "They said that. But I never meant for – "

"I know. And it's not enough." Martin's mouth looked oddly tight. "Almost isn't enough."

Julia nodded. He understood that much, at least. She could not keep living on spare love, taking the space of someone else. It was not enough.

"It's not enough for me, either," said Martin.

Julia paused.

"What do you mean?"

"I mean..." he glanced up for a moment, looking for the right words. "I mean I want you in my life as much as they do."

There was a moment of silence, hovering between them, over the snow. Julia could feel the cold working its way through the soles of her boots. She stared at Martin, waiting for him to explain himself. Surely he had not meant for that to sound the way it did.

But he was quiet. Waiting for her to speak. As though he was not sure of her response.

Had she really hidden her feelings so well?

"You want me to – to be their mother?" she said faintly.

"I could pretend it was for their sake, but I'd be lying." Martin rubbed his hand against the back of his neck, suddenly looking like a schoolboy. "Julia, I never feel more at home than when I'm with you. And I think... I think maybe if you let yourself, you could feel the same way."

Julia could no longer feel the cold. Warmth was stealing out from a point just below her ribcage, heating her toes, the ends of her fingers, the tops of her ears.

"I do," she said. "I already do."

"You do?" Martin's face lit up. Julia laughed to see how wide his smile was, joy bubbling over at the idea that her love could make him so happy.

"You do..." he repeated. "I thought I'd maybe have to talk you round."

"Maybe you could try anyway," suggested Julia.

"Don't think I won't." Martin was still smiling, almost in disbelief. Then he suddenly looked back at the schoolroom. "Oh – the boys are going to be so excited."

"You think so?"

"Yes. And my brother, he kept dropping hints that I should tell you – and my sister-in-law. Their children will love you as well. My mother will almost certainly cry, she already loves you."

"She does?" Julia felt quite dizzy at this sudden family being gifted to her, like the most carefully considered present in the world, from the most wonderful Giver.

"Of course," said Martin, as though this should have been obvious. "Which reminds me – she was going to invite you home for Christmas day, and she already warned me she won't take no for an answer."

"I'll be there," Julia told him. There was no chance she would miss it.

Home, Martin had called it. Like it was already hers, just waiting for her.

A breeze suddenly stirred, reminding Julia of how cold she was. She shivered, and Martin's brows lowered with concern.

"Come on, let's get inside before you freeze," he said, nodding back at the schoolhouse.

Despite this warning, they walked slowly along the length of the building, back towards the light and warmth waiting. Julia smiled to herself. *Home*.

THE CLOSEST THING TO HEAVEN

TERRI DOWNES

25

"I couldn't do it."

Lovina could not be sure whether Rebekkah sighed – the signal on her cell phone was wavering. She could imagine the expression on the older girl's face, however, her blue eyes rolling back, puffing out her cheeks in annoyance.

"I dropped him off with you over an hour ago – when you didn't call, I assumed everything went fine and headed back. What have you been doing since then? Standing on the doorstep? It's freezing!"

"I was sitting in the cowshed, it's heated," said Lovina, slightly abashed.

"And where are you now?"

"Walking down the road. Can you drive back from the bed and breakfast and pick him up again?"

Rebekkah definitely sighed that time.

"I can try, but the snow's coming down pretty hard over here."

"Please," said Lovina. "I'm sorry to cause so much trouble, but it's not just for me. I have to make sure Simon is taken care of. I just – I just couldn't tell them. Not tonight."

As Rebekkah agreed and hung up, Lovina hugged Simon closer to her against the biting air. She had wrapped him up carefully, but he was only a few weeks old, and she would not risk a chill.

After Rebekkah had dropped him off, secretly, Lovina had intended to walk right into her parents' home and show him to them. She had made it all the way to the back door before halting in uncertainty, wavering in the deepening twilight until her nerve had failed her and she had fled. But she had not been able to bring herself to call Rebekkah back and ask her to take Simon for another night.

Her parents had been so glad, yesterday, to welcome her back from her absence over Rumspringa that they had not noticed her tension, her jumpiness. Or perhaps they had not wanted to notice. They had not asked her about anything she had done in the year since she had been home. They had not asked her why, despite only being a couple of hours' drive away at Rebekkah's place, she had not come to visit.

Maybe they suspected something. Maybe they could read what she had done in her eyes.

They had always spoken so harshly of the youth who went away and made fools of themselves during Rumspringa. It had been hard enough to tell them, over a year ago, that she herself had wanted to go. She had made a case for her education, which had helped some, but her parents had taken the decision hard.

And now – what? Lovina was just supposed to walk into their home holding a baby and tell them to welcome their grandson?

She had no idea how they would react. This was why she had chosen to wait a day before trying. If she was thrown out, she would at least have had one more day with them. Something to remember.

Lovina looked down at Simon. He had been dozing, wrapped up so cozily, but now he was stirring. A few flakes of snow had begun to fall. If Rebekkah's worries were anything to go by, it would soon be coming thick and fast.

The road ahead and behind Lovina was dark, the last of the day's light swallowed up by the dense, low clouds.

"What am I going to do with you?" Lovina whispered to Simon.

He blinked, and looked back up at her. Lovina smiled a little. She had yet to feel that fierce maternal joy that she had always been told was inevitable with childbirth – yet she did love this little unasked-for gift. Despite all the trouble he was giving now.

It was only then that Lovina realized Simon was not looking at her. He was looking over her shoulder, at something off the road. She turned, and caught a glimpse of light through a thick hedge.

Whose home was this? Had they seen her with Simon? Lovina's heart beat faster, and she started to walk once more.

Immediately, Simon started fussing in her arms, as though he wanted her to turn back.

"Shh," she whispered. "You're to go back with your *aenti* Rebekkah. Just for another night. And we'll just have to hope that the bed and breakfast owners don't tell anyone."

Simon started to cry. He freed a tiny fist from his wrappings and waved it in front of him, still looking back at the light.

"We can't go back there," said Lovina. "I don't think that the Kaufmans will – "

She stopped.

"The Kaufmans," she murmured to herself.

The snow was increasing. Rebekkah would not make it tonight. Lovina could not return home with Simon, she just couldn't. And here she was, right outside this very house.

Lovina glanced up at the dark sky.

"*Gott*," she whispered. "*Gott,* is this right? Is this it?"

Simon whimpered. Lovina swallowed – she would have to make a decision quickly.

***

Jacob Kaufman could not remember the last time he had heard his telephone ringing. He had half-forgotten he had even had the thing installed, having only used it twice in the six years since he and Mary had moved into this house.

Now, he had had to run out through the snow to get to where it was set up in the woodshed, and when he lifted the receiver he could feel gritty dust under his palm.

"Who's this?" he asked at once, already feeling the cold through his shirt.

"Jacob Kaufman?" came a whisper from the other end of the line.

"Yes," frowned Jacob. He could not tell whether the English-speaking voice was male or female.

"You and your wife," said the voice. "You still want a child, don't you?"

Jacob found himself staring at the phone as though it could provide some answer to this mystery. He felt his stomach grow tight.

"What are you talking about?" he said. "Mary – "

"You and Mary," said the voice, "yes. You still want a baby, don't you?"

"Yes," said Jacob, his voice almost a whisper as well. "What are you – "

"Come to your front door," said the voice. "Hurry. Run."

Jacob ran.

***

Lovina counted the seconds as she waited next to the hedge. She had hugged Simon, checking that he was still warm, before leaving him in his carry basket on the front steps of the Kaufmans'. More than a minute, and she would have to go back for him.

Her heart beat painfully against her ribs as she heard footsteps inside the house.

They halted for a moment, and she took a small step forward almost without thinking.

Would Jacob refuse to open the door? Should she go back for Simon? Was it wrong to do this – in secret, like Simon was something to be ashamed of? Maybe Lovina had not heard *Gott* after all, and she was just panicking. Maybe she was supposed to keep her little gift.

But even as the thought entered her mind, the door opened, letting light fall out across the already whitening ground. Jacob Kaufman stood silhouetted in the doorway for a moment. Then he bent down.

Lovina listened as he called for Mary. She watched as Mary took one look at the little boy and caught him immediately into her arms. She waited until she saw Jacob take a few steps out into the snow, presumably to look for whoever had left the child.

Then she turned and hurried away.

***

"You just left him there? Lovina, we could have taken him to a hospital, that's what the safe haven laws are for," Rebekkah reprimanded – although she kept her voice gentle, looking at the distraught and pale face across from her.

Rebekkah had been unable to make it the previous night, and had called Lovina to let her know, only to discover that Lovina had made other arrangements. Now they were sitting over coffee at the bed and breakfast Rebekkah was staying at.

"The Kaufmans have been trying to adopt, even since before I left," Lovina said, her voice sounding as pale and tired as she looked. "Remember, I told you they even registered as foster parents, just in case? I know they'll have things at their house to take care of him. And you know Mary. You know how much she'll love him."

Rebekkah sighed.

"I haven't seen or spoken to anyone from around here since I left," she reminded her friend. "Except for you."

Lovina nodded, looking down at her hands.

Despite the pain of leaving her little boy, and despite the added difficulty of hiding her feelings from her parents, Lovina still managed to feel a twinge of another sort of guilt above it all. Rebekkah had not returned to the community since she had decided to go *Englisch* following her rumspringa. She had chosen to pursue education and a career in medicine, much to the chagrin of her family. There had been many hurt feelings, those four years ago.

Rebekkah had offered to let Lovina stay with her when she decided to use her own rumspringa to get her GED. Lovina had chosen to live at a hostel, at first, thinking that Rebekkah might prevent her from having fun. But when she thought back to that night all those months ago when she had arrived at Rebekkah's door, weeping and terrified at the knowledge of the life inside her, she could not imagine what she would have done without her friend.

Rebekkah had supported her, even helping her to complete her studies throughout the pregnancy, driving her to doctor's appointments and study sessions alike. And now, thanks to Lovina, Rebekkah was trapped back at the community that she had been cast out from.

"Maybe the roads will get cleared soon," suggested Lovina, changing the subject. "Have you managed to get hold of your manager to let him know you won't make your shift?"

"I got him on my cell," said Rebekkah, "though the landlines are down. I'm not sure when anything's going to get cleared. The storm turned pretty fierce."

Lovina remembered. She had felt grateful for the noise of it to cover her sobs late into the night.

"Why don't you come home with me?" she suggested. "I'm sure my parents will be glad to see you."

Rebekkah raised her eyebrow.

"You think?"

"Well," amended Lovina, "they know you've been helping to take care of me. They may not know to what extent, but my *mamme* mentioned she was glad I moved out of the hostel. And they're sure to be grateful to you for driving me back."

Rebekkah nodded slowly. She could not quite remember any reaction from Lovina's parents when she had left four years ago. Perhaps they would not be quite so harsh as her own parents had been.

But then, might it also not hurt if they were nice to her? She knew how badly Lovina had wanted to come back, how much she had missed her family. The two of them had not spoken of this as more than a visit, but Rebekkah knew that Lovina may yet to choose to use this as her chance return home. Especially as she had now found a place for

Simon – with a lovely, warm and welcoming family. The very thing that Rebekkah was barred from having ever again.

"I'll think about it," she said at last. "By the way, Anthony called, asked if you had decided whether or not you'd be staying yet."

Lovina glanced down at her mug of coffee.

"His grandmother probably wants me to do some work for her in the new year. I'll have to find a referral."

"I doubt he was calling on behalf of his grandmother," said Rebekkah, giving her friend a pointed look.

Lovina rolled her eyes.

"Priorities, Rebekkah."

"I'm just saying. And anyway, you didn't answer the question. Are you staying?"

There was a long pause.

"I don't know."

***

Lovina took the long way home so that she could walk past the Kaufmans'. She tried desperately to think of a reason to go in, but could think of none.

Then again, she reflected, as she trudged through the snow and stared up at the clouds that had yet to clear, perhaps it was for the best. She may not have been able to control her emotions if she had seen Simon.

It was so strange, not having her little boy with her. She felt the absence of his warmth – for months, she had carried him as part of her, and for the past few weeks he had spent most of his time in her arms. She had not managed to breastfeed him, but had held him close as often as possible anyway.

Now, it was over. So suddenly.

Was she supposed to be relieved? Or mournful?

At the moment, all Lovina felt was tired.

She tried to brighten herself up when she arrived back at home, although her guilt resurfaced at the notion of intentionally deceiving her family yet again.

Her heart ached as she entered the kitchen. It smelled just the same as it always had, and her mother looked just as she always had, leaning over the stove, a few wisps of her hair curling ever so slightly in the steam.

Esther glanced up as Lovina entered, and smiled warmly at her.

"Take a cookie," she said, gesturing. "They're just cooled enough. And there's milk in that jug. You'll be tired after your walk."

Lovina looked more than tired, thought Esther, as she watched her daughter pour herself a glass of milk and sit at the table. She looked washed out. Barely there. Not that there was nothing obvious to put your finger on – not unless you were her mother.

Not for the first time, Esther wanted to kick herself for not contacting Lovina more often during her time away. She had been hurt by her daughter's choice, but what did that matter? What could anything matter, if her girl had somehow been hurt?

It had been almost a year, and Lovina had not grown more than a quarter of an inch. She was no thinner, or fatter. Yet something had changed. Something deep.

And Esther had cut herself off from being able to ask what it was. Not now, not this soon. She had not even dared to ask whether Lovina was planning to stay for good when she had arrived, dropped off by Rebekkah.

"I asked Rebekkah to stop by," said Lovina, as though she had been reading Esther's mind. "She's trapped at the bed and breakfast until the roads are cleared. I hope you don't mind."

"I guess not," said Esther cautiously. "If she wants to. Your father did say to invite her in the other day, but I didn't get the chance."

"Oh. She wasn't sure if you would mind her coming in – after her parents were so harsh, no-one else seemed to want to speak to her either."

Lovina flushed deeply as her mother exclaimed that she would never turn away Rebekkah, that it "was not as though she had been shunned, she had never even joined the church."

She could not tell her mother the reason Rebekkah had not gotten out of the car was that she had had Simon with her.

"Oh – and Lovina, I realized that you had already left this morning when Sadie got back with the news," said her mother, turning back to the stove, "and you wouldn't have heard. The strangest thing – someone left a baby at the Kaufmans' last night."

Lovina focused on swallowing her mouthful of milk without choking.

"A baby?" she asked. "Who left it?"

"Someone dropped it on the doorstep," said her mother disapprovingly. "And on such a night, honestly, anything might have happened."

Lovina flushed. She felt an odd urge to defend herself, to tell her mother how she had made sure that the Kaufmans were home, distracting Jacob with a phone call long enough to put Simon on the step and then making sure that he was found immediately. Instead she said,

"So they have no idea?"

"None at all. You didn't see anyone strange wandering around yesterday, did you?"

"No," said Lovina. "I guess whoever it was wanted to keep it a secret."

"Well, they've done a good job," said Esther. "It can't be anyone from around here, everyone would know if someone was expecting and then somehow misplaced their child. Yet it had to be someone who wanted their baby to be raised Amish."

"Maybe someone from another community," said Lovina carefully. "Someone who had a child out of wedlock, perhaps. They'd want to keep that quiet."

"Goodness, I hope that's not the case," said Esther, laying her hand on her heart. "I was thinking it was one of those tourists that come through and get so enamoured of our ways. You think it was a Plain woman?"

Lovina shrugged. The movement felt jerky.

"A tourist would make sense," she said. "Why do you hope it's not a Plain woman?"

"Well, think on it," said Esther. "How could she hope to make a future for herself here, with a past like that?"

"Yes," said Lovina, closing her eyes for a moment. "I guess you're right."

***

Rebekkah smiled as she greeted Mary Kaufman, trying not to pay any attention to the other woman's surprised expression.

"I'm in the neighbourhood for longer than I expected," she said. "I hope you won't mind me stopping by."

Mary had not been one of the ones who refused to speak to Rebekkah when she had announced her intention of leaving, but the two of them had never been all that close to begin with. Still, Rebekkah hoped that she would be willing to let her in.

"I'd very much like to catch up with you," said Mary, still holding onto the door. "But we've something of a strange situation to be dealing with."

"I know," said Rebekkah. "I heard. I thought – well, I'm part way through my medical training now. I'm not qualified for anything, but I thought maybe – "

"Oh, you can check for any health problems, of course – thanks ever so, Rebekkah – "

The door was flung wide, and before Rebekkah quite knew what was happening, Mary was pulling her through to the kitchen.

Simon had been set up in state, with his carry basket sitting on the table and lined with extra pillows and blankets. He was cuddled up and looked well-fed, staring out at the world with his big, dark gray eyes. Just the same shade and shape as Lovina's.

Rebekkah would have thought Simon was too young to start remembering faces, but as soon as he saw her he started burbling happily. Rebekkah resisted the urge to look at Mary, in case she gave something away.

"Friendly, isn't he?" she said cautiously, making her way over.

"Oh, you can tell he's a boy?" said Mary.

Rebekkah nearly slapped her head with her hand.

"Just a guess."

Rebekkah set to a brief examination. She already knew that Simon was in perfect health, but she could not pass up the opportunity to see him one last time. She had become almost as attached to him as Lovina was, these past few weeks.

But looking around, and seeing Mary's glowing face, Rebekkah knew that Lovina had heard *Gott* just fine last night. This was the place for Simon, no doubt about it.

"Have you decided on a name?" she asked when she was done.

But at this, Mary's face fell.

"Jacob doesn't think we should give him a name."

Rebekkah blinked at her.

"Whyever not?"

"Well, he doesn't reckon we'll be allowed to keep him," said Mary. "We don't know who he belongs to – it might be that one parent still wants him, you see. Jacob's going to call the authorities as soon as the phone's working again."

Rebekkah felt her heart sinking. Why had she not thought of this? She had been caught up in the story of it all, imagining little Simon as

Moses in his basket ready to be taken in by Pharaoh's daughter, that she had not stopped to consider the legality of everything.

"Well," she said, not wanting to give Mary false hope, but unwilling to quench the small spark which remained in the woman's eyes as she looked at the child who had been given to her. "You never know."

"I guess you never do."

***

"So you're not coming back?" said Anthony.

He was clearly trying not to sound plaintive, but Lovina could practically feel him sighing over the phone. He had never been good at hiding his feelings. She had met him when preparing for her GED, and had always been able to tell how his studies were going before he said a word to her.

"I don't know," said Lovina. "I had thought that my mind would be made up for me, when I showed my parents Simon. They'd either accept him or not. But now that's not part of the question."

"I can't believe I don't get to say goodbye to him," said Anthony.

"Oh, you only met him twice," said Lovina dismissively.

"And he made a big impression," protested Anthony. "*Abuela* said she wanted to meet him as well."

"I'm sorry that she won't be able to," said Lovina, thinking fondly of the old woman who had been good enough to offer a pregnant girl work.

"And she'll be sad not to say goodbye to you either."

Lovina stayed quiet for a moment. She knew what Anthony meant by all of this – he was the one who wished for a goodbye from her – but she was grateful that he did not say it out loud. He had understood when she had told him how badly she wanted to return home. He was close to his own family, and knew the importance of such a connection. But he had hinted a few times, during her pregnancy, that he thought of her as more than a friend. Not that there had ever been a good time to act on it, with her having someone else's baby.

"Did you tell – I mean, do you think there'll be any trouble from – "

"He backed out of this long ago," said Lovina firmly. "The decision is mine."

"All right," said Anthony, his voice gentle. "Well – I've got to go. I'll be praying for you, Lovina."

"Thank you," said Lovina. "Stay warm. No forgetting your scarf at the library like always."

"I'll try to remember," chuckled Anthony. "Take care."

Lovina hung up and leaned back on the wall behind her bed. It felt odd to be making phone calls in this room.

There was so much of her new life that had felt right, and good. But being here, being with her family, made her feel as though she had been breathing the wrong kind of air for a year without knowing it.

And she could stay.

She could watch Simon grown up. Maybe one day she would be able to let the Kaufmans in on her secret, and be allowed to spend time with him.

She could begin again. Become the maiden that she was supposed to be. Marry someone. And...

Lovina shook her head suddenly. Marry someone? And what, harbour the hope that they did not mind her having had a baby out of wedlock?

She closed her eyes against hot tears that threatened to fall.

How could she have this? How was it possible?

***

Rebekkah stepped as carefully as she could across the dirt. She remembered that this particular road had often been given to puddles, and she was worried about ice.

She had managed to get through to the phone company on her cell phone, and had been told that the landlines would not be fixed until the next day. She had that much time, at least, to help Lovina decide what to do, before the Kaufmans called the authorities. Perhaps there was some way to make the adoption official, while still keeping Lovina's identity hidden from as many people as possible?

Although if Rebekkah got involved in any way, she could imagine many people jumping to the conclusion that Simon was hers. Many people had been all too ready to believe the worst of her.

She had heard of several others leaving the community before she had, but most of them still visited their homes, and things seemed to get along well enough. But they had all been young men, Rebekkah realized. It appeared that they were given more leeway than the girls.

It did not matter that she had never been in Lovina's situation. Rebekkah had done no worse than many of the other Plain youth from the area. She had dated *Englisch* boys, gone to a few parties. But rumors start easily, and her reputation was dented more than it had any right to have been. She decided to step away from the People in order to pursue what she believed was her calling in medicine; her parents had been convinced she simply wanted to spend more time running wild.

It had been hard to listen to Lovina long to return here. Rebekkah understood why she wanted it. It was like a different world, coming back. She breathed in deeply, and tipped her head back a little to listen more carefully to the silence. There were no car fumes, no echoes of televisions and music to lap at her consciousness. She missed this. She missed her family. But they had not wanted to see her again.

Rebekkah had never been baptized, and so had never broken any vows by leaving. She was not, technically, shunned. She had had every right to leave.

And yet, this was the first time she had made the short trip back in four years, knowing as well as she did that the life which had been hers had been decreed beyond her reach as soon as she had questioned it.

Was it all wrong? Was there no value in any of it? Or was she wrong – should she wish to return as strongly as Lovina did?

By the time she reached Lovina's home, Rebekkah's head was swimming. She had hoped to slip in quietly and speak to Lovina about going to the Kaufmans' in secret, but at the sound of the gate opening, the front door opened as well.

Esther waved to Rebekkah across the yard.

"Come on in," she called. "It's freezing!"

Rebekkah halted for a moment. The sight of Esther in her doorway, smiling and friendly, was one she had seen so many times before. It was enough to bring back all of her memories.

She took a moment to let them wash over her, then crossed over to the house.

****

Lovina paced the kitchen nervously.

She had come to a decision. At least, she thought she had. She had made and re-made a hundred different choices in the last hour, each time convinced that she had finally determined *Gott's* plan for her, before changing her mind a moment later.

She did not know how she would live without the love of her family. But she could not lie to them.

And she did not know how she would be able to stay away from Simon. She knew that she could not raise him – that was something she was more sure of than anything else. But she had to be able to visit. She could not remove herself from his life entirely.

Yet in telling these truths, she might be cut off from all of this. From her family. The Kaufmans might not even welcome her, once they knew the truth. What if they did not want Simon, either?

Lovina stood still for a moment. She breathed in for four counts, held in the breath for four counts, then breathed out for eight. That was something Anthony had taught her to help keep her calm before tests.

Anthony... Lovina shook her head. That was not something that she had space for in her mind at the moment.

No. She would tell her mother. Then, she would tell her father when he returned home tonight. If they could not forgive her, she would leave. She would live with Rebekkah and keep working for Anthony's grandmother, saving up for college. She might die from missing her family.

But if they did forgive her, she could stay. She would be able to live near Simon, and work in the house with her mother. She would be unlikely to find a husband, but she would have her parents and siblings. She would not be able to do the work she had dreamed of educating herself for, but someone else could do that. She could stay here, and be happy.

I can do this, Lovina told herself, as she heard her mother's voice.

Oh, *Gott,* please help me.

She was prevented from speaking when she saw Rebekkah walking a couple of steps behind her mother. But perhaps this was best, she thought, going forward to hug her friend. Rebekkah would be here if things went badly.

Lovina waited until her mother had put the kettle on to boil before beginning to speak. She wished that she could have rehearsed the speech beforehand, but never mind.

"*Mamme,* I – "

Lovina got not further. Two things happened at once: out in the barn, faintly, the telephone that Lovina's father had had installed for emergencies began to ring. And beside her, Rebekkah stiffened.

"Who could that be, calling here?" said Esther, glancing out of the window.

Rebekkah seemed to take in a big gulp of air before speaking hurriedly.

"I have to go – I have to go somewhere. Lovina, can I speak with you for a moment?"

Lovina stared at Rebekkah.

"What are you talking about?"

"It's important. We have to get to the Kaufmans' – right now."

Lovina felt her stomach flip over.

"Why?" she croaked, vaguely aware that her mother was staring at her from across the kitchen.

"Please, Lovina. We have to go right now."

"Lovina?" said her mother.

This had to be about Simon.

"All right. I'll come. Sorry, *Mamme* – "

"No," said her mother. "No, tell me what's going on. Lovina, what's the matter? You've been acting strange since you got here."

Lovina hesitated.

"I have to go, then," said Rebekkah, moving toward the door.

"Stop – Rebekkah, stop. One of you tell me, now."

Lovina took a deep breath. Four counts, four counts, and eight. She turned to Rebekkah.

"Why do I need to go to the Kaufmans'?" she asked, clearly and calmly.

Rebekkah blinked for a moment. Lovina nodded at her – giving her permission.

"Mary said that she and Jacob would have to turn the baby over to the authorities," said Rebekkah. "Without permission from the parents, they can't take in the child. They were going to call as soon as the phones started working again."

Lovina pressed her hand against her heart. No, they couldn't – Simon was meant to be theirs. He had to be.

"I'll go. I'll tell them."

She wanted to say something to her mother, but could not bring herself to look at her, and she had no time to wait for courage to appear. She ran for the door, not turning her head.

***

Rebekkah waited for a moment before looking over at Esther.

The older woman's face had gone pale.

"I'm sorry," said Rebekkah.

"I should have known," said Esther faintly, staring ahead.

Rebekkah cringed a little, waiting to hear some variation of *I should have known that you would lead my daughter astray.*

But none came.

"I should have known it was hers. The child. I was fooling myself – he arrived the day after she came back. I should have realized."

"I helped her hide him from you," admitted Rebekkah.

Esther nodded.

"Of course." Then she looked across the room, directly at Rebekkah. "That's why she was staying with you? She moved in with you – nine months ago, wasn't it? And that was the reason?"

"Well – yes," said Rebekkah. "She wasn't sure how you would feel about him. She didn't know how to tell you about what she had done."

Esther drew a shaky breath, and covered her eyes with one hand.

"Of course she wasn't sure," she said. "After all we said – after the way you were treated."

Rebekkah blinked in surprise.

She was even more surprised when, a moment later, Esther walked across the kitchen and caught her in a strong, steady hug. She returned it uncertainly.

"I should have said something," said Esther. "To your parents, or to the community, when you were cut off like that. You deserved better. And I drove my own child away, letting her think I wouldn't support her."

Rebekkah tightened her arms around Esther.

"She came back," she said. "She couldn't stand not having you in her life."

"But I wasn't there for her. You were – Rebekkah, my darling girl, thank you so much. You have no idea how much it means to me that she had you."

Rebekkah felt her throat tighten.

My darling girl.

"She's family," she managed to say.

"You're family now," said Esther. "I want you to remember that. You are my daughter now, and you will always be welcome here."

Rebekkah could no longer hold back her tears. She clutched at Esther and wept, as the older woman held on and kept her steady, pressing as much love as she could into a single embrace, knowing that there would be many more to make up for time and love lost.

***

It had been Jacob who had shown the most reservation about the child, refusing to even consider giving him a name, just in case. Yet when Lovina managed to make herself understood, explaining that the child was indeed theirs to keep and that she would see to any legalities that were required in order to make it so, Jacob was the first to catch Simon up into his arms.

Lovina watched as Jacob dropped a few precious tears of joy onto Simon's coverlet. It hurt, a little, to see someone else with such love for her child. And it would perhaps hurt more, she realized, to see Simon growing up and loving Mary in her place, and Jacob instead of the father he never would have had.

But it was right. It was for the best. *Gott* had shown her the Kaufmans. He knew.

It was a few hours before Lovina felt ready to make her way back home again. Jacob was already making plans about the adoption, and Mary had hardly stopped smiling for a minute. Lovina bade them farewell and stepped out shivering into the frigid air.

Now it was time to speak to her mother. She would have to speak to her father as well, of course, but her mother always knew what her father would say. If she had her mother, she had everything. If she had lost her, then, well. Rebekkah would drive her home when the roads were clear.

"Lovina?"

Lovina almost jumped at the sound that broke her out of her reverie. For a moment she thought that she was imagining her mother's round and smiling face, almost glowing in the wintry afternoon light.

"*Mamme* – "

Her mother pulled her into a hug.

"Seems like everyone needs one of these today," she said, as Lovina tightly returned the embrace.

Lovina wondered what she meant by that, but decided that she would ask later.

"I'm so sorry I didn't tell you," she said thickly, her voice muffled by the fabric of her mother's coat.

"So am I," said Esther. "I understand, my darling, but I wish you had known me better."

Lovina pulled back.

"You're not angry?"

Esther shook her head.

"I may have been," she said carefully. "If you had told me when it happened. And I am saddened to think on what you did, my darling. You are worth more than that. But I know that you know right from wrong, Lovina. I know that you will have thought about your decision every day while you carried your child."

"I did. I did. And – I hope you can understand, *Mamme*, but I can't regret it. I regret what I did, but I don't regret Simon. Not for a moment. You'll understand when you meet him."

Esther smiled.

"I look forward to it," she said. "Now come on home. Rebekkah did promise not to eat all of the brownies, but I don't like to leave her to be tempted."

Lovina smiled.

"She's still there?"

"We had a nice long talk, waiting for you to be finished. I thought you might want to handle everything with the Kaufmans before we spoke – but I grew a little impatient. And it will be dark soon, you know."

Then Esther glanced at her daughter, and frowned.

"Darling, you're not wearing a coat! I didn't even notice, I would have brought you one. What on earth were you thinking?"

"I was in a hurry," said Lovina.

"I hope you take better care than this when you're off working and studying."

"I always did," said Lovina.

As they walked, she saw her mother frown once more.

"Are you not going back, then?"

Lovina hesitated.

"I – I wasn't sure. I don't like being so far away from you."

"You weren't that far away, my darling. We all failed in that respect, I think," said Esther. "But you don't want to go back? Go to college like Rebekkah?"

Lovina almost tripped over a hidden tree root, she was staring so distractedly at her mother.

"Are you – *Mamme*, are you suggesting that I leave?"

Esther took a moment to answer.

"Lovina – if you want to stay, I will be very happy. But I am not certain that you would be. Please understand – I know that there is value in the way we live. You know that yourself, or you would not have gone to such trouble to give your little one to a Plain family. Yes?"

"Yes."

"And if you wanted to come back, I would fight anyone that needed to be fought in order to let that happen. You father would too, don't doubt that, although I think he will need some time to understand all of this." Esther sighed. "There would be people who would fight, you know. Not that that should stop you."

Lovina nodded slowly. She felt her mother reach over and take her hand.

"But you don't have to come back here for us to love you. I need you to understand that. The life you have made for yourself – I may not understand it, but I can see that you have been thinking on it, even in this short time you have been visiting. You had plans, didn't you?"

Esther was smiling now, making an effort, though she looked sad at the thought of her daughter leaving again.

"I – I was thinking of becoming a counsellor," said Lovina shyly. "There are a lot of girls who end up in bad situations, and they don't have the people I have had to help me through it. I thought I could turn my experience to good use."

"That's wonderful-good," said Esther, squeezing Lovina's hand. "You would do well at that."

Lovina reached up and wiped a stray tear. She was about to ask whether her mother had a handkerchief, when a movement across the pasture next to them caught her eye.

A battered green SUV was driving carefully along the curve of road that led through the center of the community, usually driven only by tractors and tourists.

"Anthony?"

The name was out before Lovina had a moment to think. Her mother looked at the car, confused.

"Anthony – is that the friend that Rebekkah mentioned?"

"She mentioned him?"

Esther turned to look at her daughter, her expression shrewd.

"She said he'd been helping out."

"Ah." Lovina felt something like a blush creeping along her cheeks. "Yes, he has. He drove me home from the hospital."

"Did he, now?" said Esther.

She raised an eyebrow, and for a moment looked oddly like Rebekkah.

"*Mamme*," protested Lovina, aware that the car was drawing closer. "There's nothing – we study together. I work for his grandmother. Stop looking at me like that – shouldn't you be telling me to stay away from him?"

Esther was almost laughing.

"I honestly don't know," she said. "It must be *Gott* helping me. And – my darling, all I can feel is relief at the moment. For the longest time, I felt cut off from you. Now you're back, I'm not going to make a fuss about your friend, especially one who has been helpful and respectful. Although – he does go to church, doesn't he?"

The car had stopped by now.

"Yes, he goes to church," Lovina hissed at her mother as the door opened. "We go to the same one."

Anthony jumped down, looking bright against the snow in a blue jacket and one of the colorful scarves that his grandmother insisted on knitting him every Christmas.

"Lovina, hi," he said, taking a few hesitant steps forward and glancing at Esther.

"This is my mother, Esther," Lovina said quickly. "What are you doing here?"

"I came to give Rebekkah a ride back, so she doesn't have to miss more work. Her little car won't make it on those roads," said Anthony, gesturing. "I went to the bed and breakfast but the woman at the desk said to try down this way."

"She's at our house," said Esther, her English a little accented. "We can show you the way."

Anthony smiled, and seemed about to accept the invitation, when he looked at Lovina again and frowned.

"You're not wearing a coat," he said.

Lovina rolled her eyes slightly.

"I left in a hurry," she said.

"And how long does it take to put on a coat? It's like thirty degrees out!"

"If I was too much of a hurry to grab a coat, when would I have had time to check a thermometer?"

Anthony rolled his eyes – he always more of a show of this than Lovina did – and started unwrapping his multicolored scarf, muttering something in Spanish.

"I agree," Esther interjected. "Or at least, I think I do. Much too cold to be wandering about without a wrap. She was raised better than that."

"I'm sure she was," said Anthony, handing Lovina the scarf. "After all the lectures she's given me about wearing a hat, honestly."

Esther then graciously accepted the offer of a ride back to the house in the SUV.

"I like him," she muttered as she passed Lovina, adding to her daughter's ever-growing astonishment. "Put on the scarf, darling."

"You can keep that one, by the way, I have plenty." added Anthony, opening the passenger door for Lovina. "For next time you go wandering about in the snow."

"I'm not a child," said Lovina, sliding onto the seat and wondering if it was worth rolling her eyes again.

"No, darling," said her mother, leaning forward from the back seat for a moment and patting her hand. "But you have people who will always take care of you. You're not in this alone. That's just the way it is."

Lovina burrowed down into the bright, oversized scarf as they drove, thinking about everything that still needed to be done. Working with Jacob and Mary, settling the adoption. Speaking to her siblings, and her father, about all that had happened and all that was going to happen. But it did not worry her.

She turned her head and peered out at the landscape as they passed. Today was already a little warmer than yesterday had been, and the clouds were beginning to drift away. The snow would be taken care of.

Soon, the road would be clear.

THE AMISH ENGAGEMENT

LORI WALL

Katie sighed as she watched her younger sister, Mary, rapped her fingers on the nightstand. In her other hand, she held her worn bible.

"Mary, please don't tap your nails on the nightstand."

"Sorry, Katie." The young girl sighed, and held the bible in both hands now. She lowered it to look at her sister. "I'm bored."

"I know it's tough to be bedridden. As soon as your leg heals, you'll be able to walk again." The community doctor had told her that as soon as her leg had healed, and she could walk on her own, Mary would be able to take off and go on her *rumspringa*. She had been looking forward to it for a year; she wanted more education.

The entire community was sure that Mary would be the one who got lost before baptism. Katie had returned from hers the week before Mary's leg was broken in a freak horse-riding accident. She had found many of the boys creepy and had almost been killed once because she was in what the locals deemed a 'bad part' of town.

At any rate, she had cut hers short by two weeks and returned home. She was to be baptized the next day, but with Mary's leg, she had postponed her baptism.

"Willis comes home today." Mary spoke up again. "You know, Mark's Willis." Katie looked up. "I hear he missed you."

"Shush, Mary. You're supposed to be reading."

"You know I can't read in bed." Her sister sighed deeply. "If you're so worried, read to me." Katie picked up her own bible as her sister continued to complain. "Hey. I'm in Leviticus."

"Alright." She managed a smile. However, as she read her sister Leviticus 2 aloud, she wasn't sure how she felt. Willis M. Wittmer had always been a bit of a rowdy boy. No one had expected him to return after his *rumspringa*, but she had always felt there was something different about him. His brown hair grew too fast for his mother to keep up with it, and so he would sometimes get away with wearing his hair longer than he should have.

Either way, everyone had been incredibly excited that he was coming home. He would be getting baptized within the week, and if Mary felt she could get on without her for about an hour, she would go. She hadn't realized she had stopped reading aloud.

"Katie?" Mary's voice interrupted her thoughts. "Katie?"

"Huh?" She looked up from the pages of the bible. "What?" Her sister laughed a little, and she looked down at the bible again. It fell off her lap, and onto the floor.

"You're daydreaming, again, aren't you?" She smiled widely. "You're thinking about *Willis*. Aren't you?"

"Am I that easy to read?" She shifted uncomfortably in her chair.

"Honey, if only I could find love that easily."

"I'm not in love." She felt her cheeks becoming even hotter than they usually were. The words came out in a mutter, and she could feel her sister's eyes on her. She didn't dare to look up again.

"Katie! You have a visitor." Their mother's voice floated up the house.

"I'll be back as soon as possible, Mary." She picked the bible up off the floor before setting it on the table. Then, she walked down to the living room as quickly as possible.

"Hello, Katie." A masculine voice echoed in her ears. Her eyes fell on a buff 18 year old with familiar blue eyes.

"Willis..." She smiled a little. "How have you been?"

"Anxious to come home." He returned her smile. "And you?"

"I've had my fair share of homesickness too." She stayed on the far side of the room. "I hear you're to be baptized soon. Congratulations."

"Thank you. Have I heard correctly that you're getting baptized soon as well?" He took a couple steps closer, but still had a lot of room to cover.

"Yes." She smiled a little wider.

"Congratulations, Katie." His smile widened as well. "I should probably get going. Is Mary still bedridden?"

"Unfortunately. How did you hear?"

"My mother told me shortly after I arrived home. She told me not to bother you much today." She couldn't help but laugh a little bit.

"Thanks. I'll see you around?" He laughed a little now, nodded, and began to walk out the door. She didn't try to stop him. However, she did notice that he had changed.

Instead of being excited about being out in the world, he had said that he was anxious to come home. Anxious to come home meant that he missed something about their lifestyle. He missed something, or someone, bad enough to forgo everything he had thought he wanted after his *rumspringa*. Not only that, but he had bulked up while he was away. Even with daily work on the farm, the men in her community weren't too muscular or strong. More often, they had the bare minimum so that they could do their job without being sore all day, every day.

He'd also grown taller. Willis had been slightly taller than her when she left; now he was about a foot taller. His smile had become a little more radiant, and he was no longer itching to get away from their lifestyle.

Katie returned upstairs slowly, thinking over his words and turning them around and around in her head. In her long blue dress, she certainly had no attractive features to show off except for the light dusting of freckles across her cheek and nose, and her light brown eyes. Her parents often said that if her commitment to their lifestyle didn't attract the boys, her eyes would.

"Who was it, Katie?" Mary tried to sit up, but groaned.

"Easy, sister." She helped her lie down again. "It was Willis."

"Mark's Willis?"

"The same." She smiled a little. "He's home, and getting baptized, as you said he was going to do."

"You should trust me more often, shouldn't you?" Mary laughed once she was lying down again.

"I guess so." Once her sister was situated, she picked up the bible again.

"Has he changed much?" The topic turned right back to Willis.

"Not so much physically. Mentally, I really think he has." Katie sat back down on the chair. "He didn't question why I was going to be baptized once; he used to question it all the time when we were younger." She smiled a little.

"Katie, are you in love?" The tone she used made her skin crawl. It felt like Mary was upset with her for almost moving on.

"Why would you say that?"

"You're blushing." Mary teased her now. "Come on, admit it. You like Willis."

"Do not." She felt a blush growing on her cheeks. "Do you want me to keep reading Leviticus or do you want some food?"

"Lunch sounds great, actually, Katie." Her sister smiled. "Do you know if mom has made any yet?"

"No, but I can go check. I might get roped into helping cook lunch, so I might be a while if she hasn't made it."

"I'll take a nap, then." She rested her head back on the pillows, letting it roll to the side. Her eyes closed, and Katie brushed some hair out of her face. She set the bible on the nightstand, and then began to walk downstairs.

The stairs creaked and refused to stay quiet. For Mary's sake, she hoped she was a heavy sleeper.

Once she was at the bottom of the stairs, Katie walked into the large summer kitchen. Her mom sat on a stool, canning a quart or so of ripe peaches.

"Mary's wondering about lunch, mom."

"You can make her something, Katie." Her mother didn't look up from canning. "Your father is out butchering the pig, and your grandparents are on the porch. See if they'd like any food. Your younger brothers and sister will be coming in with more peaches soon."

"Of course, mother." She smiled, and began to walk towards the porch. The large house made it a long walk. As she walked, she admired the well-made furniture. Her dad had made most of it by hand before she was born.

She opened the door to the porch and saw her grandmother and grandfather sitting on the bench.

"Grandma, grandpa, would you like some lunch?"

"That sounds wonderful, Katie." Her grandfather smiled, and her grandmother nodded. "Is it ready?"

"Not yet. I'll come get you when it is, though, grandpa." With that, she smiled. In this area of Pennsylvania, potatoes grew well. She decided to make a potato salad for the family, and began to gather potatoes to boil. Her mother had passed the recipe down to her last year, and the only way she would ever remember it was to make it often.

As she began to fill a pot with water, she thought about what Mary was doing. Her tone had become bitter at the end of the conversation they'd had, and she had felt rather uncomfortable. Why would Mary be so bitter?

Willis was two years older than she was. He'd often brushed her aside, not intentionally, but brushed aside all the same. As far as Katie was aware, Mary didn't even like Willis.

She sighed softly and turned the faucet off. The community here had gotten running water a few years ago, and it was such a relief. No longer did they have to warm the bath water by the stove or run outside to the pump every time they wanted water. They still used the pump, of course, to get water for the animals, but for them, they used the tap.

She set the pot of potatoes to boil as she heard the door open again. In came the rest of her siblings: Wayne, John, Samuel, and Hannah. Hannah was the youngest; at the tender age of 5, she could carry but only two peaches.

"Come here, Hannah." She smiled, and held her hands out for the peaches. Katie decided that a peach cobbler could make Mary feel a little better. "Wayne, how many peaches in that bucket?"

"Close to a hundred. How many more do you need?" Wayne was the eldest of the children, and had yet to marry. There were rumors that he was seeing a woman of 22 at the Sunday singings by the name Mary (no relation to his sister).

"Hannah's going to give me her two, so probably six or seven." As she spoke, she took the two peaches from her sister's hands gently. Wayne nodded and set the peaches on the counter.

"Peach cobbler sounds wonderful, Katie." He smiled at her before taking the rest of his peaches to the summer kitchen. Samuel and John followed suit, but did not stop to give her peaches. Hannah simply requested to mash the peaches; gladly, she peeled the peaches and put them in a bowl.

Then, she gave the bowl and a thick wooden dowel to Hannah.

"Mash away." She smiled and let her sister mash the peaches. Then, she checked on the potatoes for the salad. When they were soft, she pulled them out of the pot and began to mash them for the salad.

In all, it took her an hour to make the potato salad and stick the cobbler in the oven. She called everyone else into the kitchen and then put some on a plate for Mary.

"I'll take some up to Mary. Mom, the cobbler has about half an hour; could you pull it out when it's done?"

"I got it, Katie." John spoke up. "You take care of Mary." John was a year away from his *rumspringa*, but he had this certain quality of stubbornness. She doubted he'd be gone for long.

"Thank you." She smiled. "Tell grandma and grandpa I'm upstairs, please."

"Of course." With that, she walked two plates of potato salad up to Mary's room. Well, Mary shared it with her and Hannah. The three beds stretched east to west across the room, with a small closet to the other end of the beds. A nightstand was situated to the left of each bed for braiding strings and bibles. Flowers sometimes made it in, but that was rare.

"Mary?" Katie gently shook her sister awake. "Lunch is ready." She set one plate on the nightstand by her bed, and then she walked to hers.

"Mmm?" Mary never woke well, but today was a different story. "You made potato salad?"

"Yeah. Our potatoes haven't been stored right, so they were beginning to go bad." She began to eat her food. "There's a peach cobbler in the oven."

"Fresh peaches?"

"Yes, Mary. With fresh peaches; freshly picked this afternoon, actually."

"I guess that's what the others have been doing."

"Mom's been canning all morning, but yes. Our brothers and Hannah have been picking peaches all morning, they told me." She smiled, and watched as Mary ate her lunch in silence. The silence hurt a little bit; they were a tightly-knit community. What could be causing her to stop talking to her own sister? "Mary, did I do something wrong?"

"What do you mean?"

"You've hardly spoken a word to me other than to confirm your thoughts." She took another bite of her salad. "Did I do something wrong?"

"No. I'm very happy for you." There was a bitter tone. "Cross my heart."

"Alright..." Katie wasn't convinced, but let the topic drop. She finished her potato salad, and gathered up her dishes to take downstairs. "Are you done, Mary?"

"Yes." She almost shoved the plate at her, hardly touched. "I lost my appetite."

"Do you want some peach cobbler when it finishes?"

"No." Mary rolled over. "I'm going to finish my nap."

Katie didn't have time to object before Mary seemed to completely ignore her. She sighed softly and began to walk back downstairs. Maybe she could can some peaches before her cobbler finished.

She washed the dishes and put them away in silence. Tomorrow was Sunday; would she miss visiting and singing to take care of her sister?

Her mom came in as she was drying the plates, and picked up the utensils to dry.

"Do you want to go to the evening singing tomorrow night, Katie?" Her mom's question was a little on the nose. She nodded slowly. "Have you talked to Mary about it?"

"Mary won't talk to me." She tried not to cry. "She won't tolerate me for more than a few minutes at a time before she slips back into silence."

"When did this start?"

"This afternoon, after Willis visited." A tear trickled down her cheek, and she almost dropped the plates. Her mother took the plates and rag from her, setting them on the counter. Instead of wiping her tears away, she hugged her. Katie couldn't remember the last time her mother hugged her.

"It'll be alright, Katie. I think she's upset she can't go out into the world yet. She wants to spread her wings as badly as you did." Her mother rubbed her back as she found herself crying. "I know you haven't seen her in two years; it's natural to feel like there's a gap there."

She sniffled, eventually calming down.

"Thanks mom."

"Now, I think you should get the cobbler out. Enjoy a big piece." Her mother pulled away. "I'll finish the dishes."

She managed a smile and pulled the cobbler out. It was a little burnt on the edges, but her mother had saved it from burning too much by turning the oven off. Now, she set it on the cool counter on top of a small washcloth. Then, she began to cut the pieces. She cut it so that everyone could have a piece, though she cut Hannah's a little smaller so hers could be a little bigger.

Her mother laughed, but knew that's how they all did it. Whoever made the cobbler got the largest piece since Hannah was too young to have a normal sized piece yet. She managed a smile, and scooped a piece up for Mary. She carried it up the stairs, and then set it on Mary's nightstand. Even if she didn't want it now, she would have a piece available for her.

Then, she walked back downstairs to enjoy her piece. The rest of the family was coming in, and they all took a piece. They left the largest piece for her, an unspoken rule in the house.

"Thanks, Katie." Her grandmother smiled. "You're wonderful."

They ate the cobbler in silence. Her mind reeled, but she couldn't turn off the thoughts that her sister was bitter over Willis' attention to her.

***

Katie smiled as she put on her best clothes for the singing. It was almost six PM on Sunday evening, and her mother was going to help Mary for the night. Wayne and John were old enough to go to the singing events as well. Their grandparents would entertain Hannah and Samuel for the night.

"Are you ready, Katie?" Wayne called from the room across the hall.

"Almost, Wayne! I'll meet you at the door."

"Okay." Her brother left her alone and let her get ready in piece. She pulled her hair into a braid and quickly tied it off. She'd had enough of her hair being in her face, the stringy ends particularly.

Then, she walked downstairs. In her blue dress with long sleeves, slightly lower neckline but still appropriate, she felt as if she were going to catch Willis' attention again. Maybe it wouldn't be so bad, to have

Willis paying attention to her. She did like him quite a bit, but wasn't sure she would like to marry him.

Based on their interactions earlier, however, she knew that it'd be a good choice to marry him. He'd blossomed into a young Amish man that no woman would be able to say no to.

With that thought tucked away in her head, she arrived at the door. Wayne and John were already there, both dressed in their best clothes. Their mother waited to see them off.

"I'll take good care of Mary tonight, Katie. Enjoy your night." Her words made Katie smile. "If she wants you here, I'll come get you, but I hope you get to enjoy the night." With that, she sent them off towards the barn where Sunday evening singing was held every week.

It was a silent, ten minute walk. The silence was not like those that Mary forced upon her. Instead, the silence filled her with hope and joy; this would be quite an exciting night. She would have a chance to see other members of the community that she hadn't seen, and possibly find someone who struck her fancy.

When they arrived at the barn, the singing was up and running already. She separated from her brothers, promising to find them at the end of the event. They smiled, nodded, and agreed to it. Then, they proceeded to join in on the festivities. A long table with food sat to one side of the barn.

She migrated over to see if someone had brought cherry cobbler. While her family didn't grow cherries, plenty of other families did. The table had plenty of finger foods, and two cherry cobblers sat to one side. One had already been half eaten, and the other was untouched. She cut herself a small slice of cherry cobbler and began to eat it.

"Katie?" A voice behind her made her jump; she almost lost her cherry cobbler. She turned around, and laid eyes on Willis.

"Willis." She smiled after swallowing. "I didn't expect to see you here today."

"I could say the same thing about you." He smiled back. "Is Mary doing better?"

"Mom's watching her tonight so I could come here. If I'm needed at home, someone else will come to get me." She smiled a little more. "Your baptism was a lovely service."

"Thank you." He couldn't help but grin at her with his goofy, toothy smile. "I hope your baptism service is as lovely." She felt her cheeks heating up a little.

"Is there a reason you wanted to talk to me, Willis?" She took another bite of her cherry cobbler. Cherry juices ran down her chin, and she managed to catch them with a napkin.

"Would you like to meet up next week at the evening singing?" He handed her another napkin as he asked. She almost choked on her cobbler.

"M-Me?" She couldn't believe his words. "You want to meet up with me next week?"

"Yes." His smile turned into a slight frown. "Do you not want to?"

"N-No, I want to." She managed another smile. "I didn't think you'd ask so soon."

"Wonderful!" He smiled, a little too excited. "I hope you don't mind that it was so soon."

"No, not at all." Her voice quivered a little. "I'm worried about how Mary will react, though." Willis' brows furrowed. "Mary's been giving me the silent treatment."

"Why?"

"I don't know." She sighed, and picked a plate up to set her cobbler on. "I think it has to do with your visit yesterday. It didn't start until after you visited."

"I only visited to say hello." His brows stayed furrowed. "I didn't mean to make her think I was interested in anyone unwillingly..."

"She teased me about it before we went on *rumspringa*. Now, she teases with a bitter tone and a scornful eye." She sighed, dabbing at her cherry stained lips. "She won't even hold a conversation with me beyond making sure she knows what's going on."

"Do you think she wanted me?"

"I think it's because her *rumspringa* was delayed. She's a lot like you were before you left, Willis." She took another bite of her cobbler as the rest of the group started another song. "She wants to leave the community for good."

"I don't think she'll want to after she spends some time out in the real world." He cut himself a piece of cobbler as he spoke. "I thought I wanted to, and then I realized that it was nothing without the community. Without you." He flashed her a smile before he took a bite of his cobbler.

"Without me?" She found herself blushing again. The heat in her cheeks told her so.

He nodded slowly as he swallowed.

"Without you, I found that the women wanted to be with me. Apparently, I'm a good looker. Until they realize I won't be able to pay for everything they want, at least." He laughed. "All the girls I met wanted money."

"A lot of guys I met simply wanted me on their arm for a pretty face." She sighed, rolling her eyes. "I hated it. Eventually, I gave up and started saying no to them. One of them had ties to a gang, and...and they almost killed me. That's why I came home." In the middle of her story, her tone changed. She felt tears welling in her eyes, but she refused to cry.

"I'm sorry to hear that, Katie." Willis put a hand on her shoulder softly. "I think it was smart to come back home after that."

"Mary broke her leg the next week, and we had to postpone my baptism." She pushed tears out of her eyes softly, trying not to make it obvious that she wanted to cry.

"Katie?" A voice interrupted the conversation. "Mary's asking for you at home." Looking around, she found Samuel standing in front of her. "Mom sent me."

"Thanks, Samuel. I'll walk you home." She cut another piece of cherry cobbler before she turned to Willis. "I'll see you around, Willis."

"See you around, Katie." He smiled at her, and gave her a small wink before she led her younger brother out of the room. "I'll tell your brothers that you had to go early." She smiled.

"Thanks." With that, they left the singing and began to walk back to their home.

"Can I have a bite, Katie?"

"That's why I cut another piece, Sam." She smiled, and used a fork to cut a small bite off for her brother. "Here you go."

"Thanks!" Her brother's face lit up, and she couldn't help but smile as he took a bite of the cobbler. "Cherry?"

"Yes. I don't know who made it, but it's good, isn't it?" She took another bite after she finished speaking.

"Yes." Her brother smiled. "Are you okay?"

"Willis and I were having a conversation about our time outside the community."

"Oh. Is it hard for you to talk about?"

"At times." She smiled a little. "Tonight was one of those times, but it had nothing to do with you or Willis."

"Did you enjoy the time with Willis?"

"Yes." She smiled, brushing a loose strand of her hair behind her ear. "I did."

"Should we expect a wedding soon?" Samuel began to tease her. "Willis and Katie getting married?"

"Samuel!" She half-scolded him, but the laugh in her voice gave her away. "I don't know." She sighed. "I honestly don't know. You know relationships are never public until a wedding date is for sure."

"I know." He sighed now. "Can I have another piece?"

"Fork?" She held her hand out for his fork as they neared the porch of their house. He happily handed her the fork, and she gave him another piece. "Thank you, Katie."

"You're welcome. Share the rest of that piece with mom and Hannah, okay?"

"Okay!" He took the plate and forks before heading towards their parents' bedroom.

"And with dad if he's home." She called after him, and only got a thumbs-up in the air. She laughed, and then headed upstairs to her room. Mary was fast asleep in her bed. As quietly as she could, she changed into something she could sleep in. Hannah was not asleep yet.

"Katie, is that you?" Mary softly spoke.

"Yes. Did I wake you?"

"No." She rolled away from her. "You can go back to the singing."

"But Sam said..." She was unsure of what to do; now half changed into something to sleep in, she couldn't go back.

"Mom had to go do something; I'm fine." The bitter tone returned. "Go away."

"Mary, we have to talk about this." She pulled her sleeping clothes on the rest of the way and sat down at the head of Mary's bed. "Why are you being so bitter?"

"Did Willis ask you to meet him next week?"

"What?"

"Did Willis ask you to meet him next week?" Her sister repeated the question, but didn't look at her.

"Yes." She softly answered. "But he didn't mean to upset you yesterday."

"I thought you were going to wait until I was out to do that!" Mary almost exploded at her.

"What?"

"I thought you were going to wait until I was in the world to do that." She sniffled. "No one ever seems to care what I think!"

"Mary, that's not true, and you know it." She touched her sister's shoulder. "What do you think?"

"I want to go out." Her sister's voice quivered. "I want to be independent." At this, Katie crossed the room to face her sister. Tears streamed down her cheeks, and she was sobbing too hard to say anything.

Katie simply hugged her tightly, unsure of how to take the new development. However, the hug didn't last long. Mary pushed her away hard, sending her to the floor. She sat up slowly, her head spinning lightly.

"What was that for?" She tried not to sound upset with her sister, but failed.

"Hugging me!" Mary now yelled at her. "I don't like being touched."

"I'm sorry. I thought you could use a hug." She sincerely apologized. "Are you okay?"

"What?"

"Are you okay, Mary?" She sat on her knees, closer to the bed. "Emotionally, are you okay?"

Her sister sniffled, confused by the question. She let her sister take her time, hoping that their parents hadn't heard Mary yelling.

"I-I...I'm okay now." She sniffled again, wiping her eyes. "Do you think you'll marry him, Katie?"

"I don't know." She smiled a little. "Please, don't tell anyone."

"I won't." Her sister sniffled again. She handed her a napkin, and waited as Mary blew her nose. "I think you two make a good couple."

"Are you done ignoring me?"

"Ignoring you?"

"You weren't doing it on purpose?"

"No. I wasn't sure why you were the one watching me so often." Her sister propped herself up on her elbow, careful of putting extra weight on her broken leg.

"Because I love you, Mary." She smiled softly. "Everyone else has been helping can."

"You don't really like to can, I remember now."

"Yup." She laughed a little as she remembered the incident that had turned her off of canning. Her finger had gotten stuck in a jar or a lid – she couldn't ever quite remember which – and had been covered by scalding fruit. Her finger was still scarred from it.

"I'm sorry, Katie." She spoke in a soft voice. "I didn't mean to tear you away from the singing."

"It's alright, Mary." She squeezed her sister's hand lightly before pulling away. "Why don't you get some rest?"

"The peach cobbler was delicious, by the way." Her sister smiled. "Thank you."

"You're welcome." She smiled. Maybe this would end well after all.

***

A month and a half later, Katie stood in her room, wearing a simple blue dress with a big bunch of flowers in her hands. The weekend after Willis had asked to see her the next week, he drove her home. Wayne and John left them alone to talk, having left earlier in the evening.

Willis had made the journey to his house at two in the morning, and their friendship acted as a catalyst. It was the quickest courtship they had seen in the community in decades, her grandmother said.

"Katie?" Hannah's voice filtered up the stairs. She turned around, and saw her youngest sibling sitting on the top stair. "You wove Willis?"

"Yes. I love Willis." She smiled, and picked up her younger sister. "One day, you too will be in love. It won't be for years, but it will be soon."

"Ew." She made a face. "Me no wove boys!" Katie laughed.

"Do you like my dress?" She quickly distracted her sister.

"I do!" She smiled widely. "Katie wook pretwy!" She laughed again.

"Do you want to wear a blue dress too, Hannah?" When her sister nodded excitedly, she set her down on the bed and looked for Hannah's blue dress. She found it under the bed, and helped her younger sister change.

Mary had left to explore the outside world the week before, but was returning to see her sister get married. She would be wearing something from the outside world – a dress, she believed it was, in a greenish color.

She shook her head lightly and began to braid Hannah's hair as she hummed a hymn. They still had about an hour before the wedding was to begin. They would make visits next weekend, since they had church tomorrow. Due to the timing of the year, they were able to get married quickly.

"Is Hannah up there with you, Katie?" Her mother's voice came up the stair case.

"Yes, mother." She smiled. "She's with me."

"Katie wook pwetty!" Her sister again complimented her, pronouncing the word 'pretty' differently than she had before. It was all part of a five year old's charm, though.

"Okay; I wanted to make sure she hadn't run off. Willis will be here soon; are you ready?"

"I'm ready. I didn't think he'd be here for another hour..."

"He's going to be early." Her mother did not hesitate to say it. "He told me last night that he wanted to see you before the wedding, but I asked him not to come so early."

"It's alright, mom. Is everyone else here?"

"Everyone's early, oddly enough. When he gets here, we can start." When she said that, her nerves began to jump. She was really doing this; she was really getting married.

The door downstairs opened, and she heard her to-be husband's voice in the hallway. She sent Hannah down ahead of her, her braid wildly flinging against the air as she ran. Katie took in a deep breath, and then began to walk downstairs.

The ceremony was all that she had hoped it would be. Mary had brought a friend with her – a guy who thought he was falling in love with her. They spent an entire afternoon singing, dancing, and enjoying the community's company. For the moment, they were to stay with her family until their new house was finished. The community was going to help them work on it tomorrow, so it shouldn't take long at all.

At the end of the festivities, Katie essentially collapsed in Willis' arms. Mary and her friend had driven home. Everyone else was getting ready to go; they had a long buggy ride ahead of them to get back to her place. Willis placed a soft kiss on her forehead before helping her up and out to the buggy.

"I love you." He spoke the words first. They had yet to say them to each other, but in the quiet of the night in the buggy, he broke the silence with them.

"I love you too, Willis." She couldn't help but feel an overwhelming smile on her face. A sense of belonging took over her, and she rested her head on his chest as they began the ride home. It was difficult to find a comfortable position in the bouncing buggy. Sleeping would have to wait until they arrived home.

"Are you looking forward to having a family?" He again spoke up.

"Yes." She couldn't stop her smile from widening. "I want to have a large family. Five kids, at least."

"Five kids, at least, it is." He smiled and laughed. "It sounds wonderful. And on our farm, what shall we grow?"

"Cherries, peaches, potatoes, and anything else you can think of." She smiled. "I can farm, and you can put your carpenter skills to good use."

"Good thing I have my own tools." Another chuckle came from his mouth. It shook his chest under her, and she smiled. The silence set in again, but it was a good, comfortable type. She bit her lip softly, and pressed her head against his shoulder. He put an arm around her, drawing her closer to him on the seat.

Before she could object, he had a blanket out from under the seat and laid it across the both of them.

"Better?" He smiled down at her.

"Much, thank you." She couldn't hide her smile, even if she wanted to. "Can I fall asleep now?"

"We're almost there, Katie." He brushed some of the loose hair out of her face. "But I will carry you in if you fall asleep."

"I love you so much." Her words echoed softly in the dark night, and she closed her eyes. His arms held her closer, and she could feel the buggy bounce up and down under them.

As she was falling asleep, the buggy came to a sudden, jerky stop. Willis stopped her from falling off the bench, and picked her up.

"But I'm not asleep…"

"I want to carry you in." He smiled down at her. "Sleep. We can always talk tomorrow. You're exhausted."

"Thank you." She smiled, speaking softly. He opened the door and walked her inside. She closed her eyes again, and found herself quickly drifting off to sleep. She felt him carry her up the stairs. He set her on the bed, and she heard him shuffling about the room for a few moments.

He got in bed beside her, and she felt a different kind of material touch her skin. He'd changed clothes before he got in with her. She smiled, and drifted off into a wonderful sleep.

Tears of an Amish Widow

Erica Hennig

There were a lot of things in life that Hannah King imagined she'd be. A mother, a wife, possibly even a mentor to young women; a widow was not something she'd imagined for herself.

There was an illness running through the little Plain community. It was something like pneumonia, but the English doctors were having a hard time controlling it as well. Hannah's husband, Joab, was a farmer with a caring heart. He chose to follow the doctor around and help him however he could. Since the illness was contagious, Joab eventually became sick.

Hannah wasn't going to let this illness stay in the community anymore. She made the decision to take Joab to the actual English hospital. Though they were able to keep him alive a little longer, they still could not save Joab. Hannah was crushed, her heart felt as though it had been ripped out of her chest and beaten with a sledgehammer over and over.

How am I going to take care of our little Samuel? How will I live? Who will take care of me?

The oncoming depression wasn't one she could push away with a few good thoughts and a well-placed Bible verse. She desperately tried praying, hoping that the God she served would send a sign that everything would be alright... but nothing came. No signs in the sky, no angels to comfort, and no one to care for her and her little boy.

Ultimately, she knew that the community would take care of her for a time, but she also knew that she would have to pull herself together eventually. Especially if she was going to continue to support her son. He no longer had a father, and Hannah was determined to make sure he had a mother.

Day in and day out, she began to do what she could to care for Samuel. She worked in the local store, and sold things she knitted at the market on the weekends. Hannah would help in the schoolhouse if they let her, and they did until Samuel got to be the age that he could go to school. The community leaders decided having one of the students' parents there would cause a conflict in the community as to why a certain parent was allowed there and none others.

Just as the new school year was around the corner, the school teacher—Miss Schwartz—got married and decided to quit teaching. Hannah didn't understand how the community could let something like that happen. She went on a rampage one day and told the leaders exactly what she thought of them in the little church building where they were meeting.

"How could you leave the children with no one? Who in this community will train our children on the right path? You must have *something* in place! Surely, you're not that stupid."

She heard a throat clear behind her and saw a handsome, young man standing in the doorway. He smiled as her face flushed with embarrassment.

"Ms. King, this is Michael Fisher," one of the elders said. "He will be the new school teacher. We have decided that you will assist him for the first three weeks of classes, then you must find something else to occupy your time."

"'Occupy my time?' You make teaching sound like a hobby! Isn't investing in the next generation important to you?" Hannah felt a hand on her shoulder and she knew it was the new guy, Michael. Something about his touch calmed her, and her heart instantly ached for the tender touch of a husband again.

"Ms. King," Michael's voice was barely above a whisper. "Let them do what they feel is right. I care about the children just as much as you do. We'll work something out for you."

Hannah relaxed a little, nodded in response, then turned around and walked out of the church. She discovered that the men in that room might not have cared for the children, but the man taking over as school teacher certainly did. And she could get behind a man that was confident in what he was doing. She was going to make the next three weeks the most meaningful yet.

Samuel was so excited for the first day of school that he could hardly contain himself. Hannah walked with him a little earlier than most other students. She wanted to be there early to make a better impression than the first time for Michael.

He probably won't even remember me anyway, she thought to herself. *Almost every single girl in the community has made contact with him. I'm sure we've all started to look the same to him.* Though Hannah was afraid to admit what exactly that meant, even to herself. She hated lumping herself in with all of the young, unmarried girls in the community, but sometimes she found herself acting just like them. Of course it was only a few years ago that she was unmarried and pining for every guy that walked into her life.

Her train of thought was interrupted by Samuel suddenly dashing off toward the school.

"Samuel, wait!"

Hannah tried to call him back or catch up with him, but he had such a head start that he was in the school building before she had even crested the hill the school was standing on. Michael popped his head out of the door, probably looking for the parents of the small child who had just entered the school an entire hour before school was even to start. As soon as he saw Hannah, he smiled wide.

"Ms. King," he declared instantly.

So much for forgetting who I am, she thought as her face grew warm.

"Mr. Fisher," she spoke politely. "I just want to apologize for the way we met—"

Michael held his hand up. "No need. All is forgiven. And please, call me Michael."

"Hannah." She stuck out her hand for him to shake, but he took it and kissed it lightly instead. Her heart skipped a beat.

"The pleasure is mine," he said as he looked into her eyes. His were a deep green that fit well with the sandy blond hair on his head and tan skin she could see. Hannah thought he looked almost too tan to be a teacher, but decided the first official meeting wasn't the right time to bring that up.

"Samuel and I are here early to help you set up since it's the first day of school," Hannah quickly changed the subject before her mind went any further away from the original reason she was there so early.

Michael turned and walked into the building, ready to have a helper there.

"I'm glad you'll be here for a few weeks. Sometimes the first three weeks are the hardest on a teacher."

"You've taught before?" Samuel sounded surprised. Michael laughed.

"Of course, buddy," Michael bent down to Samuel's level and addressed him directly. "I was a teacher in another community before I came here."

"Why didn't you stay there then?"

"Because I heard there was another town that needed help, and I like a good hero story." Michael winked as Samuel's eyes grew wide.

Hannah laughed at the exchange before telling Samuel to make sure that every desk had pencils.

As the boy ran off, Hannah began to explain to Michael what they had done last year before Michael cut her off with a wave of his hand.

"I do appreciate the input Hannah, but I would like to do something a little different this time. The children don't know me, and I don't know any of them. I don't want to really come down as an overbearing teacher on my first day." Michael winked. Hannah didn't understand that logic, and she certainly didn't appreciate feeling like she was being spoken to condescendingly.

"Excuse me, sir, but I think we should at least address what the children did." Hannah was going to let him have it anyway. "The children come here to learn, not to make friends with the teacher. If you think for one second I'll let you get away with talking to me like that, you have some life choices to reevaluate." Michael's eyebrows shot up, but he didn't say anything.

Hannah continued. "You might think you're some big hot shot coming here on the invitation of the elders, but you're only here because I already have a child and they won't let parents of a child in the school be the teacher. So you can take the smug, entitled attitude and stick it... somewhere!" She turned and walked out of the building, now feeling like a bit of a moron for telling the handsome, new school teacher off. She was only outside a few minutes before Samuel came and got her.

"Mama, don't let Mr. Fisher scare you away," he spoke tenderly to her. "Besides, maybe he can help you become an even better hero." Hannah looked at her son and realized that even though she didn't think very highly of herself, he thought the world of her. And she wasn't going to let him down; not today, and not ever.

"Okay," she consented as she gave Samuel a hug. "Let's go inside and show him how it's done."

The next few week flew by quickly, and the fact that Michael had been making subtle advances wasn't lost on Hannah. She loved the fact that someone was even toying with the idea of courting her. Since it had been almost five years since Joab had passed on, Hannah didn't think any man would ever take a liking to a woman with a child.

There was only a small problem with the whole situation, and Hannah hated to admit it to herself. Abigail Miller had also shown an interest in the young Mr. Fisher. She was by far the prettiest girl in town with her beautiful blonde hair, deep blue eyes and nearly flawless skin. There wasn't much wrong with Abigail, except that if she didn't get her way she tended to have a fit. But with all of the guys in town constantly pining for her, that rarely happened. Until Michael Fisher came along.

Hannah wasn't sure if he was declining young Abigail's advances or simply playing hard to get, but it made Hannah a little nervous. She felt like there might have been something between them, but this was the last day that she would see Michael on a regular basis. Since it wasn't out of the realm of normal things she would do, she had already decided that she would walk Samuel home from school everyday. Especially if that meant she got to see Michael Fisher for a few minutes.

As all of the children were released to go home, Hannah decided to see if she could get an idea of what was going on in his head.

"This is my last day," she picked up a pencil off the floor as if it was the only purpose she had in the world. She looked up at Michael at the front of the room. He simply nodded, his face tight with emotion.

"Are you okay?" Suddenly nothing else mattered. She moved to the front of the room and stood next to him.

"I just hate it that things have to come to an end," he began to cry. Hannah was shocked. She'd never really seen a grown man cry before, and she wasn't sure what to do. She put her hand on his arm.

"How can I help you?"

"You can stay," he chuckled. They both knew that wasn't her decision and she said as much. Michael replied, "That doesn't mean you can't try to get an extension."

"I'm a woman," Hannah shot back. "They are far less likely to listen to me than they are to you. Besides, you're the teacher. You know what you need far better than I do."

"All I need is you."

Hannah froze. Did she just hear him correctly? "What?"

He pulled away. "You're right, I shouldn't have said that. I apologize." He began busying himself with unnecessary papers on the desk.

"Michael." Hannah grabbed his arm and he stopped. He looked at her and their eyes met. Tears were brimming in his eyes. She wanted to hear him say it again. "What did you say?"

"All I need is you." He turned to face her fully. Her heartbeat sped up, but her breathing became shallow. She knew this feeling; Joab used to make her feel this way. But Joab was gone, so she attempted to push all thoughts of her dead husband out of her mind.

Michael looked at her a moment longer, but he must have seen the inner turmoil because he finally said, "No." And he turned and went back to the useless straightening.

"Did I do something wrong?" Hannah's heart hurt a little as she was suddenly treated very coldly. He stopped.

"No, but I need to take this slowly. Not for your sake, but for mine. There's so much I haven't been able to tell you because we've been at school. Let's have dinner tonight. Bring Samuel. The Miller's live right next door and they have a son he can play with."

Hannah knew the Miller's well, especially because Abigail was the one after Michael's heart. This was a good sign though, because it meant that although Abigail was trying, she wasn't doing as well as she might have thought. And she wasn't asked over for dinner like Hannah. She would still be careful not to give in too much to this. There had been too many times already where men thought they wanted Hannah, but they didn't want Samuel. Since the pair were a package deal, there wasn't much option once they realized how serious Hannah was about her son.

I guess we'll find out tonight how he really feels.

As he usually was, Samuel was ecstatic to be spending any time with Mr. Fisher.

"Do we need to bring anything, Mama? I can't imagine that a *man* would cook anything well." Samuel made a face as he finished his thought. Hannah laughed.

"Samuel, don't be so mean," she playfully scolded him. "Maybe he had all sisters and learned how to cook from them. Maybe he was an only child. I don't know, but you can ask him when we get there."

The ten-minute walk seemed to be the longest walk of their lives. As they got closer, Samuel got more talkative, but Hannah became more quiet. *What if he decides he doesn't like me? How will I tell Samuel?*

Does he even like Samuel? It seems as though he likes children, but sometimes Samuel is a handful. Maybe we should turn around...

The doubting game was becoming too much. Hannah felt a hand wrap around her hand and looked down to find her son had grasped her and was smiling up at her.

"Remember Mama," Samuel said sweetly. "No matter what this man thinks of you, I still love you." She felt an unchecked tear slide down her cheek. She stopped and scooped the little boy into her arms, as they held each other and cried. When Hannah finally put Samuel down he said, "Besides, Jesus still loves you too. And He's the only man you need that *really* matters."

Hannah had to keep from crying because they had already rounded the corner onto the street where Michael lived and he was standing in the doorway waiting for them. Hannah began to apologize for keeping him waiting, but he just waved his hand as he usually did when he didn't want to hear excuses.

"Anything you need to say isn't going to make up for the lost time, so let's not waste any more with apologies." He smiled as if to say there was no need to feel bad for anything she did, though she still felt the need to apologize for apologizing before realizing that would have been counterproductive. She stepped over the threshhold behind her son and was surprised to see an almost immaculate house with the smell of roast beef, carrots and potatoes wafting throughout.

"Mama, it doesn't smell this good when you cook!" Samuel seemed to suddenly have no filter. Thankfully, Michael took it gracefully and defended Hannah's honor.

"Now now, that's not what we say to our mother, is it?" He knelt to Samuel's level, ever the teacher. "She cooks for you, doesn't she?"

The little boy nodded.

"You're never hungry, are you?"

He shook his head.

"Do you sleep in a house?"

A nod.

"Do you have decent clothes to wear?"

Another nod.

"How about some nice shoes?"

One more nod for good measure.

"Then you only say nice things about the woman that treats you well."

"Yes sir," Samuel said before Michael nodded and stood.

"Now," he clapped his hands together. "Who's ready for dinner?"

During dinner, Samuel asked every question he said he was going to, from how he knows how to cook to why is his house so clean to why does he teach. Everything seemed to be going really well until suddenly the 5-year-old had a different plan for the interrogation.

"Do you plan on marrying Mama?"

Hannah's face quickly grew warm and she studied the plate in front of her, afraid of what Michael would say. *This wasn't supposed to happen!*

Without skipping a beat, Michael replied, "Well, that really depends on her. I've already made my decision, but if she keeps pushing me away... then we'll see."

"That would be really stinky. Because Mama really likes you and she's a lot happier with you in her life. In fact, I don't think I've ever seen her this happy. She even sings in her sleep now." Michael laughed at the boy's sudden burst of random facts.

"Oh, does she?" Samuel wasn't even phased.

"Yeah. I think they're songs she used to sing with Papa, but I was a baby when he died, so I only hear stories now. But I think she told me once that was a song she used to sing with him." Samuel shrugged before adding, "Do you have anything for dessert?"

"As a matter of fact I do. Then, you should go play with David Miller next door while you Mama and I talk about grown up stuff."

Samuel seemed to like that idea, so Michael went to get the dessert. Strawberry shortcake with vanilla ice cream.

"Where did you learn how to make ice cream?" Hannah tried to keep the conversation away from their relationship for the time being. She was still reeling from the question of marriage.

"Oh that's simple stuff really... I just went to the English store in town." They all laughed. "More accurately, I have a Mennonite friend who gives me ice cream on a regular basis. It's a treat for me and not one I share with everyone. Tonight, I have two honored guests in my home and I want you both to know that you're special to me."

It was quiet for a few moments, but finally Samuel pushed his chair back and got up from the table without asking.

"I think that was my cue to leave." With that, he walked out the front door and closed it behind him.

"I can't argue with his logic, even if he didn't ask to be excused." Michael looked at Hannah and began his thought. "I've been meaning to tell you this since I met you, but I really do have intentions of marrying you... but like I told Samuel, that is entirely up to you." He sighed and leaned back in his chair. "Would you like to move to the living room? The dishes can wait until later."

Hannah was so enamored by the way Michael's house looked that she couldn't imagine that he was actually fine with leaving dishes unwashed, but she didn't argue because she knew this was a conversation they needed to have.

Once they sat down and were comfortable, Michael continued his thought.

"There is no one in this world who has made me feel more comfortable than you have. From the second I heard how passionate you were about the children until I saw you and Samuel walking up to my house with red eyes from crying, and right up until this moment; there is no one in the world I want in my life more than you and Samuel." He smiled when he said her son's name.

"Who named him?" Michael asked.

"Joab did. He was sick when Samuel was born and said that I was to dedicate him to the Lord just like Hannah did in the Bible."

"Were you having trouble conceiving as well? Actually, I'm sorry—"

Hannah laughed. "No apologies needed, and no we weren't. But he knew from the start that he probably wasn't going to make it. In some ways, it made his passing easier, but in others... it just became harder."

They were quiet for a few minutes before Michael reached out and grabbed Hannah's hand in both of his.

"No matter what anyone says or what anyone does, I will always be here and I will always make my way back to you if you ever feel like we're too far apart."

Hannah had tears in her eyes and she didn't know what to think. The only thing she could manage to get out was, "Why me?"

Michael smiled.

"Because you're everything I've asked God for in a wife, and Samuel is everything I ever wanted in a son."

"What about Abigail Miller? I thought she was interested in you." Hannah simply had to know. She didn't want there to be anymore confusion or dissension between her and the Miller's.

Michael simply shook his head. "She's okay as a person and very beautiful. But she's no Hannah King. You tend to doubt yourself, but you're more beautiful than ten Abigail Millers'. You have beautiful brown hair that reminds me of dark chocolate and rich brown eyes to match. You have cute freckles on your nose that almost seem to contract when you squint your eyes just right... and when you get embarrassed or upset, your face gets really red and it's actually kind of cute." He winked at her.

Despite the tears, she managed to laugh at the last part. She didn't know if she should be rejoicing for herself or praying for Abigail. She loved Abigail like a little sister and would rather have her happy. As if

Michael could suddenly read her mind, he pulled his hands away and gave an exasperated sigh.

"Hannah, Hannah. Why can't you just take the gift that God is giving you? Stop pushing His free love away and stop pushing me away. I'm not usually one to give ultimatums, but if you can't make up your mind, then maybe we shouldn't even try." With that, Michael stood up and went to the kitchen to finish washing the dishes. As he left the living room he called back, "When you're done in there, go ahead and let yourself out. Thank you for coming over."

It was at that moment that Hannah realized she had just potentially thrown her life away. She couldn't move from her spot as much as she didn't want to be there anymore, but she had to do something. So she got down on her knees and just began crying out to the Lord for all of the things she had done to push the people in her life away. She had never done this before, and it was weird to do it in a place that wasn't even familiar, but she knew she needed to do it and she didn't care who could see her.

She didn't know how long she was there for, but when she opened up her eyes and wiped the tears away, she noticed that both Samuel and Michael were on their faces as well, crying and praying along with her. Michael was closest to her, so she put her hand on his back. He began to shake and sob even louder.

When he finally quieted down, she put her mouth down by his ear and whispered, "All I want is you, Michael. I give myself to you."

He breathed a heavy sigh and finally forced himself up. They looked into each other's eyes and knew this was only the beginning of something much deeper than either of them could fathom. He smiled a crooked smile as Samuel sat up with tears still streaming down his face.

"Geez, if you wanted a revival meeting, why didn't you just set one up with the elders?"

Two days later was Sunday, and the town went to church as usual. Michael grabbed Hannah and Samuel on their way out and asked them to stay a few more minutes with him.

"I have something I want to say to the elders and I want you to be there when I do."

"Both of us?" Hannah asked curiously.

"Of course. You come as the whole package." He smiled at them and Samuel couldn't contain his excitement over the mysterious way Michael was acting.

As soon as the last of the churchgoers had left and there were only the elders and the trio, Michael made his move.

"Excuse me, I have something I would like to propose."

The elders looked at him curiously and the preacher said, "Go on."

"I would like for Hannah to be my assistant for the rest of the school year. I know you told her that she couldn't, but the rule that she would be partial to her son is a little silly, since I've seen her in action and she's only more strict on him. These last three weeks have been a huge transition into a position I've never really had before, and Hannah has made everything I've done seem like it was extremely easy."

"We will consider your request, but we can't make any promises," the preacher seemed to be the speaker of the elders today.

"There's also another thing that you might want to consider," Michael seemed to be struggling with this one a little more. He looked at Hannah for just a moment and she nodded, not knowing what he was going to say but showing her support in whatever was about to happen.

"I want to marry her too."

The elders went into a tizzy trying to wrap their heads around this proclamation.

"What? You want to marry a widow?"

"What about children of your own?"

"What about Abigail Miller? Surely she's the better fit."

All of these quick suggestions cut Hannah's heart like a knife, but Michael stopped them all with a wave of his hand.

"My mind's been made up. I love Hannah King and have since I watched her stand up to you almost four weeks ago. And I love Samuel. He's dedicated his life for God's use only and he's everything I always prayed I would have in a son. As for Abigail, God will give her the right man at the right time. I'm not that man, and this is not that time."

The elders simply couldn't believe what they were hearing, but suddenly decided they needed to act right then. They quickly shuffled out of the sanctuary into a back room to discuss, leaving Michael, Hannah, and Samuel alone.

Hannah started to feel those doubts come in again, but this time she stopped them before they could start. *I have a man for the first time in years that loves me like God loves me! How can I ever say no to that kind of love?*

Samuel was starting to get anxious, but Michael wouldn't let him leave, so they began playing a game of tag in the sanctuary. Hannah sat and watched them play, laughing at the way Michael looked, behaving like a 5-year-old.

After almost an hour, the elders finally emerged from the back room. Some of them looked overjoyed and others looked pensive. Hannah wasn't sure if that was a good sign, but she braced her heart for anything.

"Don't." Michael had come up behind her and must have seen her body language. "Don't close your heart. Open it up. Allow yourself to feel. How can you love if you don't let yourself get hurt once in awhile?"

Hannah wasn't sure how to answer that question, but she didn't have the time. Samuel abruptly stopped gallivanting and returned to his place by his mother's side.

The preacher spoke. "We have considered your requests and have but one condition." He looked at the three of them equally. "That you must stay in this town for the rest of your lives and give your lives to serving the children of this community. They need people with big hearts like yours, and this town needs people with new hope to bring a fresh perspective."

"Wait, I have to stay here for the rest of my life?" Samuel asked. "Can't I go home?"

They all laughed as Michael explained he had to stay in the town, not in the church itself. "Ooohhh. Cool!"

Hannah was in shock that they were actually letting this happen. "You're okay with us getting married?"

"God has ordained every man, a wife." The preacher submitted. "And God has ordained every woman, a husband. You have been blessed enough to have been ordained two husbands. The favor of God is on your life, child. We know you won't do anything that would hurt us with it."

Michael pulled her into a hug, as he was still in shock that they said yes. He began to cry into her hair as she cried into his chest. They were going to get to start fresh on everything. And it was the best feeling ever.

Abigail still came to the school everyday to see Michael. Maybe she was hoping she could change his mind, because by now the whole town knew that Michael and Hannah were courting to be married. By the end of that first week, Hannah finally pulled Abigail aside and asked her what was going on.

"I just can't believe that a handsome man like Michael would fall for a widow like you."

Hannah did all she could not to choke the woman out with a bunch of children still around. She wanted to be a good example.

"Well, my dear, I'm sorry that you didn't get your way this time. I guess when it comes to matters of the heart, you're just not the expert."

Abigail huffed, "Who made you the judge on what I'm expert in?"

"Well I know good wife material when I see it, honey. If you want I can help you hone that passion a little better so that people start to take you more seriously. Men like a woman that can really stand up for herself without looking like a 5-year-old."

Abigail looked as if she'd been accosted, but she gathered her composure enough to curtly say, "Maybe I would like that."

Hannah smiled, hoping for only the best in this situation. "Alright then. I'll see you tonight at my house."

"Tonight?"

"Yes. If you want a husband, we must start right away."

"No, I can't do tonight! I have plans."

"With?"

Abigail suddenly looked very flustered. "Someone."

Hannah's eyebrows shot up. "A boy?"

"It's none of your business!" And she picked up the dress from around her heels and marched down the hill.

"What was that all about?" Michael asked as Hannah came back in to finish getting the room ready for tomorrow.

"Abigail's been seeing someone, but she's been coming up here everyday for you. I was nice, but I basically told her she needed to stop."

"I never heard you use those words. It actually sounded as if you were genuinely interested in her life."

Hannah smiled. "It's not like I'm not. I still want to see her do well, even though in her eyes I stole the man she wanted."

Michael stopped what he was doing and pulled her into him. "Hey." He looked deep into her eyes until it felt like he was seeing into her soul.

"No one stole me from anyone. I am my own person and I make my own decisions. Take those thoughts out of your mind right now."

Hannah closed her eyes to clear her head. Suddenly she felt something on her lips. She opened her eyes and saw that Michael was kissing her! She instinctively pulled back and it shocked him.

"What's wrong?"

"Let's... do that again."

This time she was prepared. And it was a glorious kiss with so much emotion and passion behind it. Hannah wasn't sure what had happened last Friday when they were on the floor of his living room, but since then their relationship seemed to be on a fast-track. It was overwhelming at times, but in times like this it felt just right. This was the healing that she needed after Joab died.

As Michael pulled away from Hannah and they looked at each other again, she told him, "Just now was the first time I've thought of Joab in a longing way in a week. Should I feel bad about that?"

Michael shook his head. "The memories of those we loved will always be there, but we have to learn to move on. Thinking of Joab in a longing way meant that even while I was trying to make a move, you were shutting me out. And you did. Now that you've experienced some healing and given a lot of that hurt to God, there's room in your heart to love again."

He suddenly became very serious as he got down on one knee and pulled a small box out of his pocket. He opened it as he spoke to reveal a gold ring with a small diamond set in it.

"With this ring I want you to promise me that you will always be open and vulnerable to me about what's going on. That you will tell me when you're hurting and that you'll tell me when we can rejoice together."

She nodded, too overwhelmed to speak. Her vision became cloudy as he finished his speech.

"As I give you this ring, I promise that I will always protect you and lead you in the ways that God is showing me to take. I promise that I will love and care for Samuel as my own and that he will be my own son... just as you will be my own wife."

Hannah managed to squeak out a "yes" as she threw her arms around her beloved Michael and they cried.

"I love you, my crying widow." They both laughed through the tears as they knew this would certainly not be the last time they cried together.

Their foundation was built solidly on the passion of teaching children and leading each other into the deeper things of God. Hannah knew that this was the best way to start any marriage, and she was blessed to get a second chance to do it all again. This time, she knew it would be for eternity.

When Amish Love Finds A Way

Stephanie Swift

"Katherine, for the love of all things holy and good, will you please stop?"

Katherine Mills sat upright on the church pew and furrowed a brow at her younger brother, Jonah. The worship service would be starting soon, but she couldn't concentrate after discovering one of the buttons on Jonah's shirt was missing. She turned his wrist over to inspect the cuff...again.

"Why didn't you mention it this morning?" she whispered. "I could've mended it before we left."

Jonah jerked his arm from her grasp as his eyes roamed over the congregation. An elderly woman seated in front of them passed a snide glance their way, but the old gossipmonger was the least of her concern.

"Katherine, I'm not a kid anymore. It can wait. Now please stop embarrassing me."

Katherine laced her fingers together on top of her lap and turned her attention to Bishop Abram, who was slowly making his way to the podium at the front of the sanctuary. Her embarrassing Jonah? The thought nearly made her laugh out loud. Oh please...as if he didn't do an excellent job of that on his own. Katherine rolled her eyes heavenward when she caught him winking at a couple of single women sitting on the opposite side of the church.

"Really, Jonah, don't you have any manners?"

He chuckled at her remark before the Bishop garnered the congregation's attention. A hush fell over the crowd and they all bowed their heads when he started the service with a long prayer. She made a mental note to mend Jonah's shirt as soon as they returned home. Perhaps he didn't mind going out in public with tattered clothing, but it bothered her to no end. The last thing she wanted or needed was for the people in their little Amish village to think she was slacking in caring for her brother, a job she'd taken very seriously since their parents' death three years prior.

When Katherine opened her eyes, she was surprised to see someone had joined Bishop Abram behind the podium, but it was no ordinary person, and the stranger certainly wasn't from their community. The gentleman standing beside the Bishop was dressed in English clothing, sporting a short beard and mustache, and he held a cell phone in his right hand. Katherine felt her cheeks flush, and she tried not to stare, but he was quite handsome.

The congregation shared curious glances as the Bishop gestured to the man and introduced him as Dr. Steven Read, a newcomer to Lancaster, but no foreigner to the Amish. He explained how the doctor was raised in the faith as a child in western Pennsylvania, and that he'd discovered his calling in life during his Rumspringa when he was just sixteen years old. He'd practiced medicine ever since and had recently taken over Lancaster's small medical clinic after the previous owner retired from the field.

"My brothers and sisters, I hope you will join me in welcoming Dr. Read to Lancaster and to our community. Several of you have mentioned to me how time-consuming it is to make the trip to the clinic, and Dr. Read has generously volunteered to make house calls."

The excitement in the room was almost palpable and Katherine felt her stomach flutter with excitement also. She'd lost count of the numerous times she'd wrangled Jonah into their carriage and made the long drive to the clinic - sometimes in the dead of night and even during torrential downpours. As far as she knew, the previous doctor never made house calls, at least not to the Amish households, so this was a welcomed change for sure.

After the Bishop introduced Dr. Read and concluded his discussion over the services he would provide, Katherine expected the doctor to leave, but he didn't. Instead, he sat down on one of the front pews and joined in the service. A couple of hours later, when Bishop Abram asked if he'd like to close the service with a prayer, he didn't falter or try to beg his way out of it. He wholeheartedly accepted, and his prayer even received a rousing "amen" from the Bishop when he finished.

Katherine struggled in vain to keep from ogling him, but she couldn't help herself. There was something oddly fascinating about the man - and it wasn't just his rugged good looks either.

"Really, Katherine, don't you have any manners? Stop staring." Jonah mimicked as they stood to leave. Her cheeks burned a bright shade of red as she playfully elbowed him in the stomach, which made him laugh. Two of his close friends caught his attention as they waved to him from across the crowded room, and when he left her side to join them, she was grateful for the reprieve.

Bishop Abram and the doctor stood by the front door, and as Katherine watched him smile and introduce himself to each member of the congregation, she stole a glance toward the back door of the church. Unfortunately, the throng of people was too big to push through so a hasty retreat in the opposite direction wasn't possible.

"Dr. Read, this is Katherine Mills. She and her younger brother, Jonah, own and operate the local dairy farm."

Katherine jerked her head around, not realizing the fast-moving crowd had already nudged her to the front of the line. When she nearly bumped into the doctor, she took a couple of hesitant steps backward to regain her footing.

"H-hello. It's nice meeting you. Welcome to Lancaster," she stammered.

The doctor grinned and thanked her, and Katherine felt her heartrate escalate when the masculine aroma of his cologne wafted past her nose and left her temporarily dazed. He pulled a business card from his jacket pocket and handed it to her, and when their fingers touched, she held her breath.

"Please don't hesitate to call me anytime you have an emergency - day or night," he remarked.

She didn't trust herself to say anything else without sounding like an enamored schoolgirl, so she simply nodded before turning to leave. Perhaps it was just wishful thinking, but she could almost feel the doctors gaze on her as she walked away, which made her legs wobbly and sent a chill up her spine.

Katherine sighed.

She couldn't deny it. The new doctor in town had her spellbound.

* * * *

Steven squinted as he peered out his car window, trying to discern which of the small houses belonged to Miss Hannah Bowen. He glanced at his notepad again and mumbled the information he'd hastily scribbled down while rushing out the door of his clinic.

"House #142. Okay...where are you?"

It was his first medical call to the small Amish village since Bishop Abram introduced him to everyone the previous Sunday, and his stomach flip-flopped with equal parts excitement and fear. He wanted to make a good impression, but as he circled back for what felt like the hundredth time, he started to wonder if he may have bitten off more than he could chew. With the sun setting on the horizon, most of the houses looked identical in the fading light, from their brown tin roofs straight down to the white wooden swings on their front porches.

He strongly considered throwing in the towel until he caught sight of an older woman standing on some porch steps, waving her arms high in the air to get his attention. As he brought his car to a stop in front of the house, he caught sight of the small metallic numbers nailed to one of the porch columns - #142. When he turned off the ignition and stepped out with his medical bag in tow, the woman left the steps and walked around the vehicle to greet him.

"Miss Bowen?" he inquired.

She nodded and motioned toward the front door. "*Yah*, thank you so much for coming, Dr. Read. My son, William, woke up this morning with a fever, and he's been sleeping off and on all day, which isn't like him because he's usually full of energy."

He could tell by the way her voice shook that she was worried, and as they made their way inside the small wood framed house he understood why. A young man who couldn't have been more than twelve years old stood just inside the doorway, holding on to the back of a tall chair. His unruly brown hair was plastered to his skin and his face was a deathly shade of white.

"William!" Miss Bowen exclaimed. "What are you doing up?"

He opened his mouth but no words came out, which alarmed Steven right away. He noticed how William swayed precariously on his feet, and he rushed over to keep him upright before he toppled to the floor.

"Your mom is right. We should get you back to bed."

When he put his arm around William's waist to keep him steady, his heart plummeted to his feet when he felt the intense heat emanating from William's body through his clothing.

"Miss Bowen, can you please bring me some ice wrapped in a bath cloth or dish towel? He's burning up with fever and we need to get it down as quickly as we can."

Tears cascaded down her face as she directed him to William's room before racing to the kitchen. Once William was lying comfortably on his bed, Steven opened his medical bag and removed a stethoscope and otoscope so he could listen to his chest and examine his ears and throat. Fortunately, his lungs sounded clear, but his ears and throat were extremely red and inflamed, which could explain the fever.

Miss Bowen returned with the ice and placed the towel against William's forehead. He opened his eyelids slightly and moaned, and Miss Bowen kissed his cheeks and caressed them gently with her fingers.

"It's okay, sweetheart. I know you're hurting, but Dr. Read is going to help you feel better. I promise."

He appreciated her show of confidence in him, especially since he was basically a stranger to her small town, and he smiled before continuing his examination. The lymph nodes in William's neck were swollen and tender, and although the ice brought his fever down somewhat, it still wasn't where Steven felt it needed to be.

"Miss Bowen, William's ears and throat are badly infected, and I would like to give him a shot of Rocephin, if it's alright with you. This medicine will take care of his fever more quickly than taking oral medication, and I'm worried if we don't get his fever down soon he might have a seizure."

As soon as Steven mentioned giving him a shot, William's eyelids flew open and he fervently shook his head while Miss Bowen struggled to keep him still. "No, no, no...I don't want a shot..." he mumbled.

Steven reached out and touched her hand. "Miss Bowen, I know how you feel about traditional medicine, and I understand because I was raised in an Amish household, but I promise I wouldn't recommend this if I didn't feel it was absolutely necessary."

The tears kept rolling down her cheeks, and the inner battle going on inside was more than evident by the pained look on her face. He felt guilty for suggesting something he knew was against her faith, but he had to do what he felt was right for William. Whether she decided to do it or not was totally up to her, but he feared there would be dire consequences if she refused. William's eyes swelled with tears, which only added to his misery, and he swallowed hard to try and keep it together. He dearly loved his job, but there were moments when he wished he'd never left home, and this was one of those times.

"Luke! Come here please!" Miss Bowen called.

Steven heard a door open in the hallway moments before a youngster appeared in the doorway. This child looked younger than

William by a couple of years, but they were almost identical with their wavy brown hair and blue eyes.

"What's wrong with brother?" he asked. His eyes were wide and expressive as he gazed at William, and Steven felt helpless and unsure of what to say. He'd tended to many children in his line of work, but having none of his own left him at a disadvantage sometimes.

"He's sick, and I need you to get Mr. Jonah right away. Do you understand?"

Without another word, Luke turned and bolted down the hallway and out the front door.

"Jonah Mills has been like a second father to my boys since my husband passed away last year," she explained. "Maybe he can help keep William calm while you give him the shot."

Steven thought for a moment. *Jonah Mills.* The name sounded vaguely familiar, and his spirits lifted when he remembered Bishop Abram introducing Jonah as Katherine's younger brother. He'd met dozens of people that Sunday in church, but Katherine was the only person he hadn't been able to stop thinking about, especially after Bishop Abram made it a point to mention to him that she wasn't married.

A few minutes later, Steven heard the front door open and he held his breath anxiously as heavy footsteps echoed down the hallway before Luke reappeared with Jonah by his side. They were both out of breath and Jonah's face paled when he saw William lying motionless on the bed. Steven leaned over and looked behind them, hoping that Katherine may have followed, but his hopes vanished when he realized it was just the two of them.

Jonah knelt by the bed and William's eyelids fluttered open when he heard him speak. "Hey, buddy. I got here as fast as I could."

Miss Bowen reciprocated the dishcloth between different spots on William's body, from his forehead to his cheeks and downward to his chest. "Dr. Read was just telling us how it would make William feel better if he gave him a shot to bring down his fever, but he doesn't like that idea very much."

Jonah nodded as if he understood before grabbing William's right hand and giving it a squeeze. "Our baseball game won't be the same next weekend if we don't have our best hitter there to help lead us to victory. I bet Dr. Read is great at giving shots. You probably won't even feel it."

He gave Steven a stern look, as if needing reassurance, so Steven reiterated to William that he would do his very best to make the shot as pain-free as possible. A couple of tears escaped and rolled down William's cheeks, but he ultimately agreed to it, and while Jonah, Luke, and Miss Bowen showered him with words of encouragement, Steven removed the bottle of Rocephin and a syringe from his medical bag and prepared the dosage.

Although it seemed to last an eternity, the amount of time it took between turning William over on his left side and Steven giving him the shot in his hip was mere seconds, and he was pleasantly surprised when William smiled at him when it was over.

"See? That wasn't so bad," Jonah said. "I'm really proud of you, buddy. You'll start feeling better in no time."

After Steven returned his supplies to his bag, he gestured for Miss Bowen to follow him into the hallway. While Luke took over holding the dishcloth to William's forehead, Jonah regaled him with jokes that had him laughing and smiling. When Steven saw the color return to William's cheeks, he breathed a huge sigh of relief.

"I'll come by tomorrow afternoon and check on him," Steven whispered, so they wouldn't be overheard. "Hopefully he'll be feeling a lot better and he won't have to take antibiotics, but we'll just play it by ear and see how he's doing."

Before Miss Bowen could reply, there was a knock on the front door, and Steven's heart skipped a beat when she opened it and he saw Katherine standing on the other side. Her long brown hair was pulled back and tied with a white ribbon at the base of her neck, and her cheeks were flushed a bright shade of pink.

"Is something wrong?" she asked, while trying to catch her breath. "I would have been here sooner, but I was getting dinner out of the oven when Luke came by, and all I heard was "William needs you" before he and Jonah took off running. I had no idea what was going on and I ran the whole way and..."

Miss Bowen raised a hand to stop her from staying anything else, which was probably a good thing, because she appeared on the verge of hyperventilating. When Miss Bowen ushered her inside and she caught sight of Steven standing in the living room, she flashed him a bashful smile. "Hello, Dr. Read. How are you?"

Steven felt tongue-tied at first, but he forced himself to say something – *anything*. "I'm doing good. Please...call me Steven."

Miss Bowen excused herself and returned to William's room, and suddenly the room became eerily quiet and very awkward. Katherine crossed her arms over her chest and rocked back and forth on her heels while Steven stuffed his hands inside his pants pockets and tried to come up with some topic of conversation.

Why was it so difficult talking to her? It wasn't as if he hadn't talked to other women before. It was ridiculous, really, and he felt embarrassed over his lack of wisdom when it came to the opposite sex.

"How is William doing?" she asked.

Steven cleared his throat before trusting himself to say anything coherent without tripping over his own tongue. "His throat and ears are badly infected, but I believe he's going to be okay. At first, he was afraid of getting a shot, but Jonah was able to talk him into it."

His comment made her smile, and Steven's heart fluttered. She was so beautiful, and her happiness lit up the entire room. He couldn't help but wonder if she even realized just how beautiful she was.

"Jonah is a lot older than William, but they are really close."

Katherine walked over to a chair in the living room and sat down, so Steven followed suit and took a seat on the sofa across from her. He could hear the muffled whispers streaming in the hallway, and his spirits lifted when he heard laughter coming from William's bedroom.

"Miss Bowen said he's become somewhat of a father figure since her husband died," he replied.

Katherine sat upright in her seat and flattened her palms on top of her knees. She looked uncomfortable, and he hoped it wasn't his presence that bothered her. If anything, he felt more at peace talking to her than he had since his arrival in Lancaster two months prior.

"*Yah*, I think it's good for them both. Our parents passed away three years ago, and there's only so much a sister knows about hunting, fishing, and farming. I do my fair share of it, but he needs more male friends in his life to talk to and spend time with."

Steven couldn't help but envy their closeness. When he didn't return home following his Rumspringa, he ruined any possibility of seeing or talking to his parents and two older brothers ever again. He didn't regret his decision to follow his dream of becoming a doctor, but he couldn't deny there were times when he wished he could go back and do things differently just to hear their voices one more time.

The sound of footsteps on the hardwood floor interrupted their conversation a few seconds before Jonah and Miss Bowen entered the living room.

"William is sleeping," she announced. "Thank you for coming so quickly, Dr. Read. He already seems to be feeling much better."

Steven took that as his cue to leave, even though it was the last thing he wanted to do. He would've been content just to sit and talk to Katherine all night. When he stood to go, she did the same, nearly causing them to bump into each other. They were so close he could see the tiny line of freckles that danced across the bridge of her nose.

"I should be going," he said. "I need to stop by the diner before they close."

Jonah waved a hand in the air, as if dismissing his comment. "Isabelle's Diner in Lancaster? No way. You can come to our house for a proper dinner. Katherine made her famous meatloaf and mashed potatoes."

He looked at Katherine, and he could tell by the bewildered expression on her face that she was shocked by her brother's suggestion. Because of that, he thought it would be best to politely decline, but before he had the opportunity, Katherine was agreeing with him. "I think that's a great idea."

He couldn't tell if she truly meant it or not, but he didn't want to be rude and ruin any chance he might have of seeing her again.

"Umm...okay," he replied, hesitantly. "Miss Bowen, I'll see you tomorrow afternoon, but if you need me before then, please don't hesitate to call me again."

She nodded before wishing them a good evening and leading them to the door. As Steven crossed the porch with Jonah and Katherine, he couldn't help but wonder what other surprises the rest of the night would hold.

* * * *

The following afternoon, while Jonah was busy gathering milk in the barn, Katherine took her cup of coffee to the back porch so she could enjoy a few minutes of peace and quiet. She also needed the coffee to keep her awake, since she'd gotten little sleep the night before. Although dinner ended early, she and Steven talked until midnight, and the remaining hours until daybreak were spent tossing and turning when she was unable to get him off her mind.

Katherine sighed contentedly as she recalled how easy it was to talk to him and the way his laughter reverberated off the walls in her tiny kitchen and wrapped around her heart. But despite the good that warmed her soul, there was also the hard truth that he'd been shunned from his own community when he didn't return from his Rumspringa.

He was now an English man who lived by English customs, and that was something she couldn't easily ignore, no matter how wildly her heart raced whenever he was near.

"What is causing such deep concentration, sister?"

Startled from her daydream, Katherine jumped and nearly spilled her full cup of coffee as Jonah laughed and bounded up the back-porch steps. When he sat down in the rocking chair beside her, she gave him a sideways glance without trying to hide her annoyance.

"I bet you were thinking about the new doctor in town," he joked. "Am I right?"

She didn't reply, but the blush in her cheeks must have given her away, as Jonah slapped his hand on the arm of the rocker and howled with laughter. "I knew it!"

Katherine steadied her cup of coffee on her lap and looked out across the large field behind their house. Rain clouds hovered in the distance and cast a shadow over the yard, but she didn't mind the impending rain. In fact, she welcomed it. If anything, it matched her solemn mood.

"I guess you think you're pretty clever, the way you snuck past me and invited him to eat dinner with us last night."

Jonah laughed again. "Oh, come on. You know you enjoyed it. I could hear the two of you talking and laughing from my bedroom."

Katherine sighed once again. "You're forgetting the circumstances, Jonah. Even if I wanted to be with Steven, it wouldn't be possible. He's already been shunned from our way of life, so no one would accept him."

Jonah frowned. "I don't think that's true. I know he and Bishop Abram are good friends, so there might be more hope than you realize."

Katherine took a sip of her coffee and let the heat from it sink into her bones. There was a lot to consider, but she was honestly afraid to get her hopes up and risk them being trampled on. There were also more important things to keep in mind besides her own feelings over the matter.

"I'm not going to leave you, Jonah. I made a promise to myself when mom and dad died that I would watch over you and take care of you – always."

From the corner of her eye, she caught Jonah turning in the rocker so he could face her, but she refused to look at him. She knew what would be behind those brown eyes, and she didn't want to see it. She'd lost count of the times they'd discussed their future and she didn't want to hear him proclaim again how he would be fine on his own someday. Perhaps he would when he found the right woman to settle down with, but until then he was her responsibility.

"Katherine, I love you, but you have *got* to accept the fact that I'm eighteen years old and a grown man."

Katherine cocked a weary eyebrow as she glanced in his direction. "I'm fully aware of that, Jonah."

He took off his hat and propped it on top of his knee. "There's no way I could ever properly thank you for everything you've done for me, but I want you to be happy. That's all I've ever wanted."

Katherine took another sip of her coffee. "But I am happy."

Jonah reached out and laid a hand on her arm, causing her to stop rocking and look his way. He had the sincerest expression on his face – something she wasn't used to seeing, since he spent most of his time cracking jokes and doing his best to make her laugh.

"I'm talking about the happiness I saw last night, Katherine. I didn't miss the way your eyes lit up when Steven was here, and I don't want you to risk losing that over me. Father taught me everything I need to know about running his business, and I can take care of myself and this farm."

Katherine let her eyes sweep over the property before she shook her head. "There's no way you can handle this all on your own."

Jonah's lips curled upward into a sly grin. "Who said I would be alone? I do plan on getting married someday, and I even have my heart set on someone special right now. I have for quite a while now."

Katherine sat up straight in her seat, nearly spilling her coffee again. "Really? Who is she?"

Jonah rested his head against the back of the rocking chair and grinned. "Don't even try and change the subject. We're talking about *you* – not me. You'll find out soon enough."

Katherine couldn't help but wonder who he was referring to, as she carefully considered every single woman in their community. There were several who came to mind, but she knew he wouldn't divulge his secret no matter how hard she pushed, so she decided to let it pass – at least for the time being.

"So, what do you think I should do?" she asked. "Should I talk to Bishop Abram first to see where he stands with us seeing each other?"

Jonah looked up at the tin roof and shook his head. "I think you should follow your heart. What do you *want* to do first?"

Katherine smiled. That was an easy question. "I want to talk to Steven and see if he feels the same way about me."

Jonah grabbed his hat and jumped to his feet. "That's what I was hoping you'd say. You should do that...*now*."

Katherine nearly choked on her coffee. "What? I didn't mean right this second."

Unfortunately, he wouldn't be swayed. Jonah took the coffee cup from her hand and disappeared inside the house. When he returned a couple of minutes later, the cup was nowhere to be seen and he had an umbrella hooked over his forearm.

"Take this in case it starts raining on your way to the phone."

He pulled Steven's business card from his shirt pocket and handed it to her, along with the umbrella. Katherine looked toward the dark clouds in the west and frowned. What if she didn't make it back before it started pouring rain? The phone shanty was a mile or so from their home, and the storm clouds were approaching fast.

Katherine stood up straight and squared her shoulders. No, it was now or never. If she kept waiting she would lose her nerve...and she would never hear the end of it from Jonah. Katherine opened the back door and grabbed her rubber boots, which were nestled in a corner just inside the doorway, and slipped them on before she changed her mind.

"Wish me luck!" she called to her brother, as she bounded off the back-porch steps and walked hurriedly toward the main dirt road. Her heart pounded furiously inside her chest, but it was a wonderful feeling – a mixture of excitement, anxiousness, and hope all rolled into one.

She prayed out loud as she walked, which bolstered her confidence. She refused to believe that God would bring Steven into her life only to break her heart by keeping them apart. With any luck, Bishop Abram and the others would be on their side as well.

* * * *

Steven unlocked his front door and retreated inside his house. He'd managed to get his groceries from the store to the car before the rain started, but now he had to carry them from the car to his house before the paper bags turned to mush and his groceries spilled all over the driveway. He groaned as the fumbled for the light switch. He didn't even own an umbrella.

Steven pulled his cell phone from his jacket pocket and plugged it into his charger on the kitchen counter. He'd noticed the voicemail icon blinking while driving home, but there wasn't enough battery life remaining to check it. He did see on the caller ID that it was the number to the Amish village, which was strange. He'd visited William Bowen around noon, and he was doing much better, so it couldn't be his mother calling.

At least, he hoped it wasn't. Steven's heart sank when he considered the possibility William may have relapsed. He quickly got the groceries inside as he waited for the battery to charge, and when he finished putting the items away, he saw a green light blinking on his phone, signaling that the battery was charged enough for him to check his messages. When he heard the voice on the other end of the line, he was taken by surprise.

"Hello, Steven. I...I've never left a message before, so I don't know if I'm doing this right or not. First off, I'm okay and there isn't an emergency. I apologize if I'm being too forward by calling you, but...I just wanted to let you know how much I enjoyed our conversation last night..."

His heart skipped a beat. *Katherine.* There was a long pause, but he could hear a loud noise in the background that sounded like thunder, and Steven frowned when he pictured her in the village's small phone shanty while the rain poured outside.

"I know our lives are very different, but...that hasn't stopped me from thinking about you. I really don't know what else to say other than I hope to see you again...soon."

Click.

Steven glanced at his wristwatch as he gathered up his cell phone and car keys. Going by the timestamp on his caller ID, fifteen minutes had passed since Katherine's call. As he raced to his vehicle, he silently prayed that the emotion he heard in her voice was the same as he'd felt since the day he met her. She was right about their paths in life being completely different, but he hoped that wouldn't stand in the way of something he felt in his heart could be very special. He'd grown up with the same Amish values and traditions, so there was no denying it could possibly be an uphill battle.

Steven roared the car to life and took off toward Katherine's house. The rain had died down to a drizzle, but the dirt road leading to the village was slippery and sent his wheels spinning. He took his foot off the accelerator and tapped his fingers impatiently against the steering wheel. He wanted to get to her as quickly as he could, but he also needed to get there in one piece.

As he neared Katherine's driveway, he caught sight of her walking across the front yard to her house. When his headlights shined upon her, he noticed how the small umbrella she carried did nothing more than protect her face from the rain. The rest of her was soaking wet.

Steven parked the car and took off on foot to meet her. She stopped when she saw him coming, and when he put his arm around her waist and led her toward the front porch, she didn't object. Just as he guessed, she was soaked to the skin and she shivered so much her teeth chattered. He opened the door and ushered her inside, and while Jonah went to the kitchen to get her something warm to drink, Steven grabbed a blanket from the sofa and draped it around her shoulders.

"What in the world were you thinking, Katherine?" he murmured. "You're going to catch your death of cold…"

She stopped him mid-sentence by placing a hand against his chest. "If you got my message then it was worth it."

Steven ran his fingers through her wet hair and moved it away from her neck, letting his fingertips glide softly against her neck. "I did."

Jonah returned with a steaming cup of coffee, but the moment he saw them huddled close together, he placed the cup on a table beside the sofa and excused himself from the room – but not before winking and grinning at them both.

Steven pulled the blanket tighter around Katherine's shoulders. "You should change clothes before you get sick…doctor's orders."

She laughed softly and the beautiful sound melted his heart and weakened his knees. When she took his hand, and led him toward the sofa, he followed like a love-struck teenager. Once they were seated, he picked up the coffee mug and encouraged her take a couple of sips. The color returned to her cheeks, although a bit slowly for his liking, and his first concern was getting some heat coursing through her veins.

"Steven…am I crazy for thinking this could turn into something more than just friendship?" she asked.

He squeezed her hands and moved closer. "No, I don't think that's crazy at all. I know we haven't known each other long, but I feel the same way. Do you remember me telling you last night how I wished I could go back and do things differently – how I never would have left my family?"

She nodded.

"I feel very strongly about that, and I know the odds may be stacked against me, but I really feel like Bishop Abram and the community will give me the opportunity to return to the fold when they see how I feel about you. All we do is pray over it and hope for the best."

When Katherine leaned into him and gently kissed his lips, he was caught off guard, but happily so. The moment may have been brief, but it left his heart racing wildly in his chest.

"We'll get through this together," she replied, emphatically.

Steven nodded – more certain in his conviction than ever before. He knew deep in his heart they were meant to be together...and he was ready and willing to do whatever it took to make that dream a reality.

Amish Decisions

Samantha Collier

Rachel looked out the window, watching the fierce blizzard swirl around the farmhouse. It had been building for days.

Last night, it had intensified so much that her sleep was disturbed. The old house creaked and moaned as the wind picked up. She had risen to her bedroom window, amazed at the snowflakes swirling as if in a vortex. The cold had punctured her skin like a million needles.

This morning, it was worse. She watched, anxiously, as her father battled alone through it, securing the animals as best as he could.

Two day until Christmas. The world was white, and frightening. Somehow, nature reflected her inner turmoil. She had not been herself, these past weeks.

Sighing, Rachel wrapped her shawl tighter around her shoulders. The temperature had dropped, again. The fire roaring in the corner seemed to throw out little warmth. At least they had enough firewood to outlast the storm. How long could the blizzard last? Would Christmas still go ahead?

Suddenly, she heard her father shouting outside. What was wrong? She craned her neck to see, but the swirl of white was so intense outside that it was impossible.

The front door opened, sending in a blast of snow. It was her father, of course. But as Rachel turned, she was shocked to see two figures with him. Both tall. One was dressed in black, in the typical Amish fashion. The other wore jeans and a huge snow coat, in the English style. Two men, covered in snow, stomping their boots onto the mat.

Her father struggled to shut the door against the wind. Then the trio walked into the living room.

Rachel gasped. How could this be? For she knew the two men. They were as different from each other as chalk and cheese. As far as she knew, they didn't know each other. How was it that they were together, in her living room?

And worse, stuck together in her living room. For this blizzard was here to stay, at least for today. There was little indication that it would abate. The two men were marooned with her family at their farmhouse. The neighbours were miles away in either direction. And the roads would be blocked.

It was as if they had planned it, but how could they have?

Two men. Both known to Rachel. Had God planned it? He knew the decision that she had to make. Had he put both here to make her decide?

***

The Amish man was Abraham. She had known him forever.

She remembered the first time that she had seen him. They had been children, going to school together. Someone had pulled her *kapps* from behind as she sat at her desk, making her cry. Well, she had only been five years old. But the boy that she had been told to sit next to reached over and gave her his handkerchief. Through her sobs, she had turned and looked at him.

"Are you alright?" he whispered, looking at her in concern.

She nodded, slowly. Her sobs abated.

"I'm Abraham," he said. "Don't worry, I'll look out for you."

And he had. Abraham had been like the brother she had never had. In the playground, he would watch her, making sure she was okay. They rarely played together, but she knew he was always there. Like a guardian angel.

They had grown up, as children must. She was always conscious of him in her life. His eyes would shine when he looked at her. A constant, like the moon and the stars in the night sky.

Rachel could pinpoint the moment when it had all changed between them.

Rummspringa had happened. Rachel had been curious about the world, and travelled to stay with English friends in the city. She had seen so many wonderful things; the English world intoxicated her.

Should she stay in her community, safe and loved, or should she spread her wings wider? What did God intend for her life?

She had met him in town, when she had returned. Literally ran into him as she crossed the road to do her shopping.

"Abraham!" She had been joyful, to see him again. But he hadn't smiled back.

"Rachel." He inclined his head, quietly assessing her. "I haven't seen you for a while. Where have you been?"

"Oh, Abraham," she gushed. Her eyes shone in excitement. "I have been to the city! It was wonderful. So many things to see and do."

He had frowned, slightly. "*Jah,* it can be exciting," he had replied. He looked her over. "You've changed, Rachel."

"Have I?" She twirled around, inviting his admiration. But it wasn't forthcoming. His statement hadn't been a compliment. She felt her excitement puncture slowly. Why was he so disapproving?

"Well, it was nice to see you," she replied. She didn't smile at him. "I must go, now. Mamm is waiting for me."

He had bowed again, and walked away without a backward glance.

And that was it. She hadn't talked to him much since. A distance that could not be bridged had sprung up between them. She heard that he was courting Eva, a girl they had both gone to school with. She had been sad that they hadn't remained friends, but philosophical, too. For her world had changed entirely.

David, the English man in her living room, had happened.

She had met him on *rummspringa*. He was a friend of the family she had stayed with. She had been shy with him, at first. She hadn't met many English men. But he had been gentle and sweet with her, asking how she was enjoying the city. Then he had invited her to see the latest exhibition of an artist that was showing at a gallery.

She had hesitated, just for a moment. But then she had accepted.

He picked her up in his car, whirling through the city streets. She wasn't used to cars, and felt quite giddy.

They had walked through the gallery together, admiring the paintings. She didn't know much about art, but David was well informed. He pointed out how the artist had used texture and shading to build the paintings. He knew a lot about the history of art, and the influences in the paintings.

She hadn't said much. It was like she was a sponge, soaking in all the knowledge that was being heaped upon her. It was fascinating, and alluring.

Could she become a part of this world?

But then, *rummspringa* had ended, and she had returned home. Her afternoon at the gallery with David acquired the aura of a pleasant dream. She knew it had happened, and that it had been wonderful. But she had not seen him again.

Until he had unexpectedly visited her.

Mamm had been shocked when she opened the door on the tall English man that day.

"*Jah?*" she had inquired, looking him up and down. "Can I help you?"

David had smiled. "Yes, I was wondering if Rachel was here," he said.

Rachel had heard his voice and come to the door, amazed. "It's alright, Mamm," she said. "This is David, a friend of the Baileys. I met him on my stay there."

Mamm had raised her eyebrows, but let him enter.

David had walked into the house, a bit awkwardly. She had made them coffee; her mother had left them to talk alone in the parlour. Rachel was mystified. Why was he here?

It turned out that David had friends in the area, and knew she was close by.

"I was wondering," he said, looking at her carefully, "whether you would like to see the gallery in the nearest town. And then maybe, get a coffee?"

Rachel had considered. She was very fond of David, but he was an Englisher. Would going on outings with him encourage him to think that she might court him?

She didn't even know, herself. It was like she was being pulled in two directions. One path, very clear and obvious – getting baptised into her community, and living the life her family wanted her to. The other path was thorny, and wound into complicated areas – to not be baptised, and so become a part of the English world. Her father had started pressuring her recently about it, to make the choice. He also wanted her to consider marriage.

I'm only nineteen, Rachel thought to herself, a bit desperately. Why must I make a choice?

But she did. If only she could be like her best friend, Lovina, who was very sure and comfortable about staying within the community. But then, Lovina had courted several local Amish boys, and knew how to talk to them. Lovina wasn't shy and nervy, like Rachel.

Rachel took a sip of her coffee, thinking deeply. David needed an answer. He had sought her out, and besides, it would be impolite to refuse him. And she did like him, very much.

"I would love to," she replied. David smiled.

She very much felt like she was on the edge of a precipice, where one wrong step could see her careering into an abyss.

***

Rachel looked at the two men, frozen from the blizzard. She could feel her mouth open, like a gaping fish. Surprise had rendered her speechless.

Abraham spoke first. "You look surprised, Rachel," he said. "I was travelling along the road when I saw a car broken down."

"Yes," David continued, looking at Abraham, "my car suddenly broke down. The electrics I think; the lights were dimming and the radio flickering on and off. Luckily, Abraham happened by and gave me a lift in his buggy."

"But the blizzard caught us, and your farmhouse was closest," Abraham continued. "So here we are."

Both men looked at her, expectantly.

Rachel roused herself. "Please, sit down," she said. At least her powers of speech had returned. "I will make a pot of coffee, and inform my mother. She is sewing in her room."

Abraham and David sat down, looking at each other warily. You could cut the air with a knife, Rachel thought darkly.

They would all just have to make the best of it. At least until the blizzard cleared.

***

As Rachel made the coffee, she thought back to the week before, when she had gone into town with David to the gallery.

It had started out perfectly fine. They had perused the gallery, and Rachel had enjoyed it again. She was getting a stronger sense of art in the English world; was becoming infected with David's passion for it. Once again, the world seemed to shift and slide for her. She could – if she made the choice – do this all the time.

But what of her family? They would be devastated if she decided not to be baptised. Oh, it wasn't the same as if she left them after being baptised, she knew that. She wouldn't be shunned. But she would still be forever separate from them. She would be able to see them, but she knew it would never be the same.

Yet, the siren's call of the gallery beckoned her. A life, perhaps, with this man? Where they could talk about art, view it, travel together?

She was getting ahead of herself, of course. She didn't know how she felt about David.

It seemed she didn't know anything, anymore. The confusion, the push and pull of it, was like a fog within her brain.

     TERRI DOWNES

They had a coffee afterwards, where David had spoken enthusiastically about the exhibition, and the artist.

"Would you like to come with me to another?" he asked, his eyes shining. "There is one in the next town starting next week."

"Maybe," Rachel had replied, frowning. "I'm not sure."

"Didn't you enjoy today?" he asked quickly. He seemed to really want to hear the answer.

"*Jah*, it was wonderful," she said. She paused, trying to gather her thoughts. "It's just that I am confused. I don't know if it is the best idea, doing this too much. It lures me away from my community."

He nodded, seeming to understand. "But then you can make an informed decision, can't you?" he pressed. "The more knowledge you have, the more power."

"Maybe," she replied, sipping her coffee. "Or maybe it is more temptation." She smiled, then shook her head. "I will let you know, David."

The shop bell rang, and someone walked through the door. She turned to look.

It was Abraham.

Would he acknowledge her? He barely spoke to her, anymore. It was sad; she remembered when they had been friends. Must everything change?

He had seen her. He paused, as if considering if he should approach.

Her heart lifted when he turned in her direction, heading toward the table.

"Rachel." He nodded at them both, his eyes widening slightly as he assessed David. Was he terribly shocked to see her here, having coffee with an Englisher? Would he disapprove?

"Abraham," she said, smiling widely. "It is so good to see you! This is my friend, David."

The men shook hands. Rachel could see David was quietly assessing Abraham, as well.

"So," Abraham said. He shifted awkwardly. "Have you been busy?"

"We've just been to see the latest exhibition at the gallery," Rachel replied. "Oh, you would love it, Abraham! Such beautiful paintings."

Abraham nodded, slowly. "I am glad you enjoyed it," he said. "Well, I must be off." He tilted his hat, at them both. Then he turned to the counter, to order what he had come in for.

"An old friend of yours?" asked David.

"One of my oldest," answered Rachel, a little sadly. "But we have drifted apart, lately. He doesn't want to be friends with me anymore, it seems." She looked down at her coffee, biting her lip.

"Well, he doesn't deserve you, then," said David, reaching out to put his hand over hers.

She stared down at his hand, covering her own. Was it seemly, especially in public? But she didn't move it.

And it was at that moment that Abraham turned back to them.

He frowned, looking at their hands. She could feel tension zip through his body, making him stand straighter. Almost as if he were about to pounce.

She quickly removed her hand, blushing. What must Abraham think of her?

The moment seemed to stretch on, forever. David locked eyes with Abraham, who stared him down. Tension filled the air.

Eventually, Abraham had broken it. He had simply turned and walked out of the shop, not looking back.

Rachel's eyes filled with tears. She couldn't bear him thinking badly of her. But what could she do now?

***

And now they were both sitting in her parlour, awaiting coffee. Life was strange, Rachel reflected as she picked up the cups and took them into the waiting men.

Her father had re-joined them, and was in the process of throwing a log onto the fire. It hissed and crackled as it fell, shooting out sparks up into the chimney. Inside, all was warm and bright; outside, the world had turned to white, a swirling vortex of snowflakes. The old house creaked and groaned under the pressure.

Rachel looked at the candles adorning the windows. The Christmas baskets, that had been prepared for the elderly in the community by her mother, were sitting on the floor, awaiting delivery. Would they be able to deliver them, now? It was only two days until Christmas. Rachel's heart constricted at the thought that those baskets would not get to their recipients in time.

Abraham was still sitting, staring at the fire and chatting with her father. David had stood up, and was looking out the window. He was frowning.

"It doesn't look like I'll be making it home for Christmas," he said, a little sadly. Rachel walked up to him, smiling.

"It might clear," she said, staring out. "I have seen blizzards suddenly blow themselves out. You might still make it." She pondered the thought of spending Christmas away from her family. She simply couldn't imagine it. She pictured them all gathered, eating a huge roast chicken with gravy and all the trimmings, just like they always did. Afterwards, there would be pie.

Christmas was about family. She shuddered. If she decided not to get baptised, she would no longer be a part of it. She couldn't bear the thought.

She could feel Abraham's eyes on her. Was he disapproving of her, again? Why had he suddenly decided that he didn't like her anymore? It was so perplexing. To have been so close to him, for so long.

They made stilted conversation as the day wore into the night. Her mother made up the spare bedrooms, and eventually they had all retired for the night. Rachel breathed a sigh of relief; she was glad to have escaped.

In bed, she pondered further. Eventually she turned to her bible, seeking comfort. A verse from Proverbs leapt out at her: "Trust in the Lord with all your heart, and do not lean on your own understanding. In all your ways acknowledge him, and he will make straight your paths."

She reflected. Perhaps there was her answer. She had been trying so hard to solve the dilemma, on an intellectual level. Perhaps she needed to stop thinking, and start trusting God. If she calmed her mind enough, he would lead her where she was supposed to go. She needed to stop fighting so hard.

She sighed, frowning. In the confusion of the two men staying unexpectedly, she had forgotten to get herself a glass of water before bed, as was her habit. She got up, sliding on her slippers and dressing gown, padding quietly down the stairs.

She had just turned on the tap and was filling the glass when she heard a sound behind her. She turned. David was standing there, looking at her.

Rachel instinctively tightened the belt on her dressing gown. This wasn't good; she was in her night attire, and didn't have her prayer *kapps* on. He shouldn't see her like this. She took the glass, smiling slightly at him as she walked past him.

He grabbed her arm, making her turn around to face him.

"David," she said, under her breath. "What are you doing? You are hurting me."

In response, he gripped her arm tighter, pulling her against him. The glass wobbled precariously in her hand. She didn't like the way that he was looking at her, not at all. What had suddenly come over him?

"Rachel, I want to kiss you," he said. Her eyes widened, in horror.

"No," she whispered. "It's not proper. This is my home, and you must respect our rules. I don't know how I feel about you, David. I know I like you as a friend."

He let go of her arm, suddenly, so that she stumbled backwards. Water spilt from the glass, slopping onto the floor.

"I should have known," he hissed at her. "You've been leading me on, all this time. Don't act innocent."

"I have not!" she replied. The accusation stung her. "You wanted to spend time with me, as a friend. That's what we've been doing. I never led you to believe anything else!"

He looked at her, witheringly. Then he turned and walked out of the room.

She leaned against the kitchen bench, breathing heavily.

What had just happened? She couldn't believe it. This was David, who had been nothing but kind and tender with her. Where had this sudden anger toward her come from? What had she done wrong?

Her eyes filled with tears of confusion and hurt. She had wanted to be part of the English world, had been dipping her toes into it. It had seemed expansive, full of things she wanted to explore. But this...this was a side of it, that she didn't like at all.

Was there truth in David's accusations? She had no idea. She was used to her community, where things progressed slowly and in sequence. Perhaps things were done differently in the English world. How would she know, after all?

Shaking slightly, she slowly walked back upstairs to her bedroom, climbing into bed. She had asked God for an answer, to lead her to decide. Perhaps, he had done just that.

But the fact remained: how on earth was she going to face David, in the morning?

***

Rachel stared out the window the next morning, breathing a sigh of relief. The blizzard was over. They were no longer stuck in the house.

She walked outside, grabbing her basket as she went. She needed to collect the eggs. Half of her hoped that David would be gone by the time she got inside. She didn't think that she could look him in the face, again.

Contradictory thoughts raced through her head, chasing each other. On the one hand, she felt anger toward him. How could he have done what he did? But on the other hand, she felt like she must have done something to provoke it. Something that she had no awareness of.

Her eyes filled with tears, again. It was better that she remain out here, amongst the hens. She didn't think that she could trust herself around anyone. She might burst into tears at the slightest thing.

The girls had not laid very many, of course. They never produced much, in winter. She could have completed the chore quickly, but she lagged.

She heard a noise, behind her. Her heart was gripped with fear. It wasn't David, was it?

But no. It was Abraham, walking up to her. "*Gutentag*," he called.

"*Gutentag*," she called back. She could feel her voice shake. She needed to get herself together.

"You are taking your time," he said, frowning as he looked in her basket. "Not many, today." He paused, looking at her. "I just wanted you to know, your friend David has left. He said he was in a hurry, and couldn't say good bye to you." Abraham frowned. "He was acting strangely, or stranger than he usually acts, at any rate."

Rachel's eyes glimmered with tears. She bit her lip. Don't say anything, she told herself fiercely.

"Rachel," Abraham said, softly. "What is wrong?"

She sat down, abruptly. Abraham sat down beside her.

"It's nothing," she said, wiping her eyes with the back of her hand. "I'm just being silly. I slept badly last night."

He said nothing, just let her catch her breath. But his eyes narrowed.

"Rachel," he said. "Look at me."

She turned her face, reluctantly, toward him.

"What did he do to you?" he whispered. "I'll go after him, this minute."

"No!" She reached out, laying a hand on his arm. He looked down at it.

"Then tell me what is wrong," he said.

"It's just a misunderstanding," she said. "David thought...that there was an expectation in our friendship. I had to tell him there wasn't. He wasn't happy – that is why he left this morning, so abruptly. He obviously didn't want to speak to me."

"What happened? Did he hurt you?" His face was dark.

She laughed, a little tremulously. "Oh, no," she whispered. "Not physically, anyway. He hurt my feelings, but that's okay. I should have known better."

"What are you talking about?" He said, frowning. "Known better than what? Rachel, the only thing that you should have known was to stay away from that man. I know you think that I don't like him just because he's English, but it's not that. I could tell what kind of man he was, straight away. He was trying to take advantage of you."

Rachel hung her head. The tears that had been threatening spilled over.

"Don't cry, Rachel," he said, gently. "I can't bear it, to see you like this."

"What can't you bear?" she cried, suddenly. "Why do you even care? You haven't been my friend in a long time, Abraham. Why should you suddenly decide what is good for me, and what isn't? Friends don't treat each other like this. Friends are there for each other, through thick and thin."

Abraham's hands balled into fists. "I couldn't watch it," he said, slowly. "I couldn't watch what you were doing. Toying with the English world. I thought you were going, Rachel. I thought you were making the decision to leave our community, and it made me so sad."

He took a deep breath. "And then, when I saw you hanging around with *him*." He spat the word, as if it was something distasteful. "I knew straight away what kind of a man he was. But you had stars in her eyes, talking about art and life away from here."

Rachel got to her feet, grabbing the basket. "Well, isn't that nice," she said. "I would never have done that to you. Friends are supposed to be there for each other, regardless of what is happening in each other's lives. But you aren't a real friend, are you, Abraham? You are one of those fair weather variety, only around when the going is good."

"How can you say that?" His voice was raised. "I have always been there for you, looking out for you when we were at school! I have been a better friend to you than most. The only time I have turned away from you was when I thought you were leaving me!"

He was panting. Rachel felt tears welling, again. What was the point of this? They couldn't communicate, anymore. They had grown so far away from each other. It was sad, but it couldn't be mended, obviously.

"The blizzard has cleared," she said. "I think you need to leave, Abraham."

She walked past him, refusing to look at him.

No, she had no idea of anything, anymore. She had lost two people who she had thought were friends. One of them she had been losing for a while, anyway; it had been a band aid she had been frightened to rip off, for fear of the pain. But in the end, she got the pain anyway. The other was a quick pain that would keep hurting, for a while at least.

There was no avoiding pain, that was obvious. You might try to dodge it, walk around it, or ignore it, but it would follow you, whether you liked it or not.

She prayed silently as she walked. She had been full of confusion about her life, and what she would do. At least now, one path was gone. She would not be keen to experience the English world, again. She was out of her depth, and besides, the incident with David had made her realise how dear her world was to her. She didn't want to lose it; not now, not ever.

She would talk to her father. She had made her decision; she wanted to be baptized into the faith.

She thought of Abraham. No, he hadn't followed her. She knew he wouldn't. He had made his choice, a long time ago. And she didn't want to be friends with someone, anyway, who couldn't accept her for herself. The good sides of her, as well as the bad.

It was all for the best.

***

Rachel sat beside her best friend Lovina. It felt good to re-connect with her. She hadn't seen her in a long time, since she had been busy with David.

The two girls were inside, next to the blazing fire. The roads had finally opened, and Christmas had come and gone. Lovina had called around to Rachel's house to deliver her Christmas present.

Rachel's eyes shone when she ripped open the small present. In her lap was a handmade crocheted rug. Rachel threw her arms around her friend.

"Thank you," she whispered, tears in her eyes. She hadn't lost all her friends.

"You're welcome," Lovina said, smiling. She had already opened Rachel's present to her, a knitted scarf. It was wound around her neck.

"You can take it off, you know," Rachel said, gesturing to the scarf. "It must be hot wearing it inside!"

The two girls laughed. Then Lovina looked at her friend. She could tell something was bothering her.

"How is David?" she asked, gently. It was as she thought. At the mere mention of the name, Rachel bristled and blushed.

"What happened, Rachel?" Lovina took her friend's hand.

"Oh," Rachel tried to smile. "We had an argument. He thought something that wasn't true about me, and didn't believe me when I told him he was wrong. It doesn't matter."

"I thought that might be the case," said Lovina, looking at her friend tenderly. "Dear Rachel, you are so shy and unsure around men. Sometimes, they misunderstand things. Especially in the English world, or so I have been told." She paused, looking at Rachel. "Have you made a decision? Do you want to stay in the faith?"

"I do," answered Rachel. It felt like a weight was lifted off her shoulders, just saying the words. She felt lighter, somehow.

Yes, the incident with David had been the catalyst, but it was more than that. God had shown her all that she stood to lose if she embraced the English world. As far as Rachel was concerned, the price was far too high to pay.

"I am so happy," said Lovina. She clutched Rachel's hands, tears in her eyes. "I don't know what I would have done without you. And I know that I am not the only one who feels that way, Rachel."

"What do you mean?"

"I am talking about Abraham." Lovina looked at her friend, gauging her reaction. "He has been so troubled, watching your forays into the English world."

Rachel scoffed. "I think you are mistaken, Lovina. Abraham doesn't care for me, any longer. He made that very clear after the blizzard. He was never a real friend."

"Rachel, how can you be so dense?" Lovina looked at her friend, her eyes widening. "It's because he is a real friend that he was so concerned! But there is more to it than that. I think he has stronger feelings for you, Rachel."

"What?" Rachel looked at her friend as if she had just started talking in another language. She shook her head, vigorously. "No, you are mistaken. If he felt that way about me, why wouldn't he have told me? And why would he just cut me off?"

"Because he was hurt, Rachel," Lovina replied. "He thought you were rejecting our faith and him, in the process. It was too much for him; he felt like he had to turn away completely." Lovina glanced sideways at Rachel. "That's what I believe, anyway."

"No, you are wrong," said Rachel, frowning.

She stood up. "I might just get a glass of water," she said. She walked to the kitchen, thinking deeply.

Lovina's words were swimming around in her brain. They made no sense to her. It was as if her world had tilted sideways. Could it be true?

And how did she feel, if it was? Abraham had been a constant in her life, as stable as the sun and the moon in the sky to her. She had assumed that he would be there, forever. It had hurt her immeasurably when he had withdrawn from her. As if the sun had dimmed, and the moon had stopped shedding its luminescence.

As if her world had stopped.

***

At least her parents were happy. That was something.

Rachel had told them her decision to join the faith, and they had been overjoyed.

"We were so worried about you," said her mother. "We thought there was a strong chance that you would join the English world." She had clasped her daughter's hands, her eyes full of tears.

Her father had nodded, pleased. "I always knew you would make the right decision," he said. "Rachel, the world is full of wonders. But your place is here, with us. I am glad that God has shown you the right path."

She was feeling a bit better about the incident with David. She accepted it for what it was, and that she had misjudged him. She had been swept away by the world he offered, for a little while. It was as simple as that.

Now that she had made her decision, everything was clear. Except, maybe, what had happened with Abraham.

She realised that she loved him. She always had. But he had turned away from her, so there was no hope for them, now. If only she had realised sooner. Maybe they might have had a chance.

Rachel walked to the end of their property, thinking deeply. She was happy that she was going to be baptised, but she was also sad. Sad for a lost love, that had never developed.

She heard a noise behind her, and turned around. The snow was still deep; although the sky was clear, she hadn't expected anyone else to be out here.

A dark figure loomed before her. She had to blink twice, thinking that she had conjured him from her imagination.

For in front of her was Abraham.

Yes, it was really him.

"Rachel." He walked toward her, not smiling. "Your mother told me you were out here, taking a walk." He paused, struggling for words. "I need to talk to you. I feel that you have misunderstood me, and I can't stop thinking about it."

She looked at him, snowflakes brushing his dark winter overcoat and black hat. Her heart swelled. If she could stand here, like this, forever, just looking at him, she would be happy.

"Abraham." She stared into his eyes. Was it possible? Were Lovina's words true?

Abraham sighed, deeply. "Will you walk with me?"

"Of course," she said.

They turned and started walking, together. She glanced at him sideways, trying to judge his mood. But he was still silent, gathering his thoughts.

Eventually, he stopped and turned.

"I know it is useless," he blurted. "But it doesn't matter to me, anymore. I have tried for so long to stop feeling this way. I know that you don't feel the same way. But I can't deny it. I have to at least tell you."

Rachel's heart stopped, just for a moment. Her breath caught on the cold wind.

"Rachel, I love you," he said, his eyes pleading. "I have loved you forever, and I will never stop loving you. I haven't told you, because I saw that you weren't ready. You needed to go off and explore the world. I was trying to give you space, to find yourself."

"Oh, Abraham," she gasped. "I had no idea. I was so hurt when you refused to be my friend, any longer. I just couldn't understand."

"It hurt me too much," he whispered, "to see you. Knowing that I loved you. And then when you started seeing David, I thought that was it. There was no chance at all." He paused, taking a deep breath. "I wanted to respect your decision. Even though I knew that he didn't deserve you."

Rachel's eyes filled with tears. "Abraham," she whispered back. "I was confused. I wasn't sure where I belonged. But I have made up my mind, now. My place is here, in our community."

He smiled, for the first time that day. It was beautiful to her. "I am so glad," he said.

"And my place is with you," she continued, facing him. "I am sorry it has taken me so long to realise it. I love you, too, Abraham. I always have, and I always will."

His smile spread wider across his face. His eyes glimmered with tears. "It is more than I hoped for. I can't tell you how many times I have dreamed of this moment." He paused. "Rachel, will you be my wife?"

The tears that had been threatening spilled over. "Oh Abraham, nothing in this world would make me happier," she breathed.

Her heart was overflowing.

It had taken her a while, to get here. To find her place in her community, and realise her love. But it had been worth it, the journey. She wouldn't take back a moment of it; not the soul searching, or the confusion. She wouldn't even take back what had happened with David.

Because it had all led her here, to this moment. As God had planned, all along.

THE END